THE SONS OF CROSBY BOOK 3

KATHI S. BARTON

This is a work of fiction. Names, characters, places, and incidents are products of the author's imagination or are used fictitiously and are not to be construed as real. Any resemblance to actual events, locations, organizations, or persons, living or dead, is entirely coincidental.

World Castle Publishing, LLC
Pensacola, Florida
Copyright © Kathi S. Barton 2018
Paperback ISBN: 9781629899411
eBook ISBN: 9781629899428
First Edition World Castle Publishing, LLC, June 11, 2018
http://www.worldcastlepublishing.com
Licensing Notes
Cover: Karen Fuller
Editor: Maxine Bringenberg

Chapter 1

Cody watched his food spin in the microwave. He didn't remember the last time he'd had a hot meal before coming here to stay, much less enough to fill his belly. Looking at the little table that Elliot had brought for him to use, he thought of all the times he'd sat at his own table, his mom sneaking bits of meat to him so that he'd have some too. Watching his dad have a full meal while he was made to watch him had made Cody all the hungrier.

His mom was dead, and he knew not only who had done it, but also how. Cody tried really hard not to think about it and the things he'd had to do afterwards. But there were times, like today, that they would come into his head and he'd not be able to think of anything else.

The sound of a great crash had him turning stopping the microwave and grabbing the little phone that had been left for him to use. He had no idea what had caused the sound, but he'd rather be hidden than not. No telling when his dad might think to look in here for him. The greenhouse, he knew, wasn't all that secure.

"Boy, where the fuck are you?" His best friend and dog, Buster, came to hide with him when he heard his dad's voice. Buster had been hurt by him too. "I'm talking to you, shit for brains, and you'd better answer me."

Cody opened the phone and looked at the numbers there. He was crying now, and he wasn't sure he was going to be able to press the right buttons. For some reason, he knew that he'd only have a single chance at calling for help, and he pressed one of the buttons.

"What the fuck do you want? Its five in the morning, moron." He didn't know the woman's voice that answered, but he didn't care. "Did you hear me, fucktard?"

"I'm at the greenhouse. He's here." The woman's voice changed after that, and he could hear her talking to someone else. Cody was afraid that he had a wrong number and tried again to tell her how scared he was. "He's here, and I don't wanna die."

"You're not. Just stay hidden, Chase and I are coming." He didn't know who that was but figured that if the number was in the phone, it was someone that would really help him. So long as it wasn't put in it wrong, he guessed. "We'll be there before you know it."

He surely hoped so. As it was right now, his dad was screaming for him to come in and he could hear him breaking stuff. Mr. Elliot was sure going to be mad when he got here. Cody would have to tell him that he could help him clean it up. If he got to live that long.

"You're trespassing, you fucking idiot. Didn't anyone ever

tell you that when you have to break a fucking door to get in, you're probably not going to be all that welcome?" Cody knew it was the woman on the phone. She sure did cuss a lot. "The police have been called, mother fucker, and you're going down."

"My kid is in here and somebody is going to pay. I saw that mutt of his yesterday, then he disappeared. I'm guessing that somebody in here is going to jail and it won't be me." The woman laughed, and then he heard the strong voice of a man. Cody wasn't sure what he was saying, but he wasn't any happier with his dad than the woman was. "I don't give two shits about this being private property. My fucking shit for brains kid is in here, and I want his fucking ass home. Now get him before I have to hurt you two while I'm at it."

This time he heard the man. "Yes, you go ahead and try that, then we'll see who gets hurt. Besides, aside from the fact that you're an idiot, what the hell do you think gives you the right to assume that you can break in here to have a look around? As you've been told, several times, this is private property." If his dad spoke, Cody didn't hear him.

Just then, Elliot appeared and put his hand over Cody's mouth. "We have a plan." Cody nodded and stood up when Elliot asked him to. "I promise you with all that I am, he will never harm you. But I want you to go out there and show yourself. My brother and sister-in-law will be out there to help you."

"He'll kill me." Elliot reminded him that his dad was only human, and they were all vampires. "Okay, I can see that. But if you guys kill him, and I would if I was one, then I got nobody at all. I mean, he's a terrible man and the worst father of all, but he's all I got now. Maybe I should just—"

"Don't say that, all right? You'll have me. And my family. Do you have any other relatives?" He told him about an aunt that lived in New York. "Good. We'll contact her when your dad is in jail. Then when he's there, we can help your mom out of being wrapped up under your porch."

Cody thought he'd rather stay under the bed for the rest of his life than go out there where his father was. His dad was a mean person, and Cody hadn't had to do much wrong to have his dad wallop him but good. But he did trust this man. The week that he'd been here, with Elliot's knowledge, he'd gotten to meet a nice woman, had food all the time, and he was clean. Brandy had seen to that for him too.

She took him to her house for the afternoon so that he could get a shower and something that didn't come from a zapper, as she called the microwave. Also, she did his laundry and gave him cookies and fruit so that he could eat that instead of the things that were bad for him. And she gave him the best hugs a little boy like him could have ever needed.

Getting up, he took a long breath in and let it out slowly. He had very little reason to trust anyone. There were people, he knew, that were nice, but in his small experience, they were all mean and hit hard. But not Elliot. He was the nicest man he knew. Cody also knew that his dad would call him a pussy, or some other bad name, just because he could. And he also knew that Elliot or any of his family could kill his dad without much effort.

"He will never touch you. I promise you, Cody. Never."

He believed that Elliot would try to make that happen, but he also knew his dad. Nodding once to the man who meant the world to him, Cody made his way out into the greenhouse and looked at the damage that his dad had done to get to him.

Why? What reason did he have to break up so many things that didn't belong to him? He knew why—because he could. That's what he told Cody all the time. He said that if people didn't want their shit broken, they should take better care of it and not put it out where he could break it. Like it was their fault or something.

"There you are, you shit for brains. You're going to get your ass blistered for this." It wasn't just a threat either. His dad had burned him before on his butt by sitting him on a hot pan he'd heated up on the stove. "You got chores that I expect you to do, too. I don't care how bad you're going to be hurting. Your mom, she ran off, and you're going to take up her slack when I—"

Cody wasn't sure what made him feel so brave. It could have been the two people that were in front of him with his dad, or the man behind him that put his hand on his shoulder when his dad started to speak. But he knew, for now, this might be his only chance to get his mom some peace.

"She ain't run off and you know it." His dad turned a dark red, like he was planning to explode or something. "You tied us to the chair and you put tape over my mouth. Then you put a big plastic bag over her head and made it real tight. I could see her face, I could hear her screams. Then you made me wrap her up in a tarp and put her under the front porch when you killed her. You said she'd be there until you could have me dig a hole to put her in when the dirt was unfrozen. Why would you do that to my mom? What right do you have to just kill someone like that? Huh?"

The woman, she told him her name was Emerald, knelt down in front of him. He didn't want her to turn her back on his dad and told her that. She only smiled at him, and Cody had a feeling that he should warn his dad not to mess with her. She was scary even with her pretty smile.

"Is your mom truly under your porch?" Wiping at the tears that he shed when he thought of how much he missed her, Cody nodded. "And you know for a fact that your dad is the one that killed her? And that he made you witness it?"

"He tied us both up and told us that he was going to teach us a lesson." His dad growled, like he did right before he came after Cody for something. But Emerald told him to just look at her. "Dad killed her, and he was gonna kill me too, but I ran off with Buster. After I had to wrap her up. It hurt me so hard to have to of done that to my own mom. You know?"

Cody watched as the woman stood up in front of him. He'd never in all his life felt like he wasn't going to be hurt by anyone until then. Mr. Elliot was behind him, the woman stood in front. And for some reason, he thought that he'd be more afraid of her than the men if he was his dad. But he was beyond stupid, Cody only just realized, and he'd get himself killed if he didn't smarten up. Cody also knew that his dad thought he was smart already, and that would be the end of him.

The sirens started blaring about the time his dad was backing away from Chase. He was a big man too, and Cody was sure that he worked out all the time. Not like his dad said he did, working out by beating him and his mom, but in a real job. Chase seemed to grow bigger when his dad told him to get out of his way.

"I wouldn't leave here if I were you." His dad asked Chase

10

why not, he'd done nothing wrong. "You see, that's where you're wrong. We've had someone watching your home since young Cody showed up cold and hungry here. If not for the quick thinking of my brother, I'm sure that you would have had him joining his mom under the porch, too. Wouldn't you have?"

"I don't know what you're talking about. And if you want him, he's yours. Got no use for him anyway. All he does is whine about shit and don't carry his weight around the house." Chase just looked at his dad and laughed. "You got no reason to be acting like you're better than I am. I just came here for my boy. Whatever he's told you, it's a lie. He's a liar and a thief too. I changed my mind. I'll take him now and we'll forget the whole thing. That way I don't have to hurt you too."

Two police officers came into the greenhouse and asked Elliot if they still needed them. Cody wasn't sure what that meant, but Elliot told them that he was going to let them take care of this. He thought that Cody had had enough death in one lifetime. The officers nodded and walked up to his dad.

"Mr. Wayne, you're under arrest for attempted murder as well as child endangerment. Those are all we can hold you on for now, at least until we can get out to your house and have a look around." Cody's dad said he'd not tried to murder anyone, yet. The officer nodded and pulled out his handcuffs. "You'll come along easily, Mr. Wayne, or I swear to you I'm going to leave you here for the Crosbys to deal with. And trust me when I tell you, I'd not screw around with any of them. They're the sort that takes care of their own and protects them in ways a human can't. They deal with threats quickly and without any kind of fanfare."

Cody looked up at Elliot when the hand on his shoulder tightened. His eyes were all bloody looking, and he could see his teeth—fangs, Cody guessed they were called—showing on his lower lip. Then when he shook himself, like Buster did when he came in out of the cold, he looked down at him with a wink and a smile.

"My stepmom, Brandy, is here. You know her, she's come to get you sometimes." He nodded. "I want you to go with her to her and my dad's house. You can trust them as much as you do me; you know that, don't you?"

"Yes, she's a nice lady. I like her. But you're not going to be hurt, are you, Mr. Elliot? You're a nice man, but my dad, he's not so nice, and he is mean when he doesn't get his way." Elliot knelt down to his level, and Cody had the overwhelming urge to hug the man. And when he did, wrapping his arms around his neck, Cody cried. "Don't get hurt. Please? You're my only friend in the whole wide world but for Buster. And he don't count much—he's a dog."

Cody was carried to the door and handed to Ms. Brandy. She bundled him up in a blanket and took him right to the car. Mr. Franklin was in there too, and he asked him if he'd gotten any breakfast with this baloney going on.

"No, sir. I was heating me up one of them breakfast logs as Elliot calls them when I heard my dad." He nodded and said they'd gotten none either, but they were up for it. "I don't have any money to go out with you. I'm sorry. Mr. Elliot said he'd pay me today, and I guess he forgot."

"He'll get around to it, you can bet on that. But you don't have to worry none about paying, son. We got you covered. Any man that can stand up to a bully like you did your dad, then he deserves a big man breakfast too. Took guts to do what you did, and now they're going to be able to find your poor momma and help her too." He didn't think they'd be able to save his mom, but he nodded at him. Ms. Brandy told him that they'd get her to a place she could be buried. Cody understood that.

He surely wouldn't want to have these people mad at him, he realized. They were good as a family, the best he'd ever seen, but they sure could be mean when they thought someone was hurting another. And Cody was sure they'd fight for him too. For the first time in his young life, he felt loved and safe. His mom had loved him, but she was gone now.

~~~

Elliot was barely holding onto his beast right now. The woman, Rose Wayne, was just where Cody had said she'd be — wrapped up in a tarp that wasn't even in that good of shape, and still with the plastic bag over her head. He wondered what sort of monster could do that to his wife. Not to mention, make his son watch. Elliot sat on the back of his truck and waited for the police to finish up. It was that or go to the jail and kill the man responsible for this.

"You going inside with me?" He nodded at Joey Williams, the chief of police. "All right. But you keep your hands to yourself until I say you can touch. I know what you're going in there for, and I have to tell you, Elliot, I'd not do it again if I didn't have to. The place is a mess."

"He might want some pictures of his mom. Wherever Cody goes after this, he'll still remember her." Joey told him again not to touch anything. He looked at his friend, and thought it was odd that he was being so firm about this no touching thing. "Is there something that you're trying hard not to tell me?"

"The boy, how long has he been hiding out in the greenhouse?" Elliot didn't answer him. That would be considered kidnapping if his dad had a good attorney, and it was common knowledge that he'd known he was there. "The reason I ask is, there is another body under the porch. It's pretty far back under there, and we might not have seen it had it not been for the tarp being shiny. I don't think we want Cody's dad to know we found him for now. He's not related to this family, but a little fella all the same. He looks like he might have been killed in the last couple of weeks."

"If he was put there in the last week or so, Cody might not have seen him. He has been with me, as you know. And the only reason that he came out of hiding even then was because he was starving. I'm betting that he's been gone for some time, at least a couple of weeks or more." Joey nodded and sat beside him on the truck. "Who is it?"

"One of mine. Pack. He's been missing for a couple of weeks too. I'm not sure what happened to have him ending up under the porch, but I'm thinking that Duncan might have thought he was killing his son. And it was too late when he figured it out once he'd already started on the— Just don't touch anything, all right?" He asked him why he'd think that about the death of the boy. "Emerald did some looking around in Duncan's head for me. He's got some nasty shit up there, she told me, and he might not make it to the cell I have all planned out for him. She wasn't all that nice about her search either."

"She is rarely nice, so you know. I love her to pieces, but she scares the living shit out of me most of the time." Joey laughed when he did. "He has to stand trial for this, Joey. You know that

14

as well as I do. If he comes up missing and people find out that I'd been harboring his son, it might not go over well for either of us."

"I told her that. She's got them little dragons of hers watching him. I'm to understand from your dad that they're not all cute and cuddly at all either." He said that they weren't. "I don't suppose, while I'm thinking about it, your family had anything to do with the baby vamps out on Sixty, did they? If you won't answer me I understand, but thanks if you did."

Elliot nodded. He still had trouble thinking about how the young vampires had been dealt with. The little dragons weren't all that cute and cuddly, not by long shot. They were big and dangerous. Deadly too.

When Joey asked him if he was ready, he nodded and made his way to the little house. As soon as he was on the porch, where the bodies had been found, he could smell it. He looked at Joey when they both stopped before entering the house.

"I'm going to ask you again not to touch anything." Elliot nodded. "I have to preserve the crime scene with this one. By the books. If your fingerprints show up here, I'm going to have to have you arrested as well, just so we don't fuck this one up. We're even recording everything from the time we got here. I sure hope to Christ that we got it all. And as much as you scare me, being a vamp and all, I don't want to have to explain to Emerald that your arrest is only temporary, until we get it sorted out."

"What am I walking in on, Joey?" Joey looked out beyond the house to the tree line. Elliot did the same. "The family?"

"Yes. They've been here since I called them to let them know that we'd found Tim, their son. The child did not go easy,

15

so you know, and it happened inside." Elliot nodded. "Is there anyone else that this kid Cody has to go to? I mean, he's going into the system if there isn't anyone to take care of him."

"He mentioned an aunt in New York." Elliot glanced back at the house before continuing. "Joey, are you all right? I promise I won't touch anything if you'd rather not go in again."

"I have to. That's the only reason I am. And with you there — well, I feel like I need someone else to witness this. Just to say that it's as bad as I thought it was the first time. And Elliot, it's as bad as it gets in there." Elliot nodded. "I'm truly sorry about this."

The scent of blood hit him. It wasn't fresh either. As soon as his eyes adjusted to the darkness of the house, he looked around. For the first time in his entire life, something sickened him to the point that he thought he would throw up. Christ, the kid had fought hard, he realized.

He had no idea how the young pup had died, but he surely tried his best to come out the winner in the fight for life. The furniture around the first room was broken and shattered against the wall. Blood was splattered all over the walls and curtains, as well as anything around the room that was out in the open. Elliot stared at the place where he was sure the boy had been murdered and stood there for several seconds just looking at the wide dark brown stain. He glanced at Joey when he said his name.

"You all right?" He nodded, then shook his head. "Yeah, just the way I felt the first time, and now too. What sort of sick fuck is this man? To do this not just to a kid that turned out to not be his, but to his wife too. I cannot wait to see him go down for this."

The rest of the house was the same. Blood marred every surface in each of the four rooms. The bathroom, where they both thought that Duncan had cleaned himself up after the deed, had been left to look like a massacre had taken place. The shower stall was stained in blood. The soap that lay on the small shelf looked like a block of red blood.

Two towels were lying on the floor. They looked as if he'd not used much water to clean himself up, but just used dry towels instead of using water first. Elliot could see him doing that—thinking that he'd just wipe it off, then when that hadn't worked, cursing as he got into the shower. Duncan's torn and bloodied clothing lay in a heap on the floor next to the tub. Even it, Elliot thought, appeared as if someone had bled all over the surface of the tiles on the floor and walls.

"He realized about halfway through that it wasn't his son, I would guess by the looks of things. He was violent at first, as you can see, but he got more so as it went on. I don't know how he got Tim in here—drugs, I'm thinking. Or he hit him on the head and wrapped him up to bring him in the house. But once he realized that he had the wrong boy, he tried to cover his tracks by killing him. The kid didn't give up either. At least that's what I'm seeing. How about you?" Elliot said he could see that. "I didn't know why he didn't call out to his parents in this. They would have gladly come for him. But when I talked to them about finding Tim, they told me that he'd only been seven years old, and he wasn't old enough to call on his wolf yet. It's a real shame I can't let them take care of this for us all."

They wandered through the house. It was sitting on a slab, so there wasn't a basement that could've held more blood and secrets. The latter Elliot had decided he wasn't keen on seeing, if there were any. As it was, Elliot wasn't sure that he'd sleep well tonight. Not after this.

There were no pictures of Cody's mom. Nor were there any of the young boy. No things hanging on the refrigerator that Cody might have made. There wasn't a single item in the house that made him think that a kid lived there except for the blankets in the corner of a room and a small pile of dirty clothes. Elliot felt his beast stir under his skin at the monstrous acts of some people. Emerald contacted him just as he was coming out of the house.

There are two things that you should know, one of which is going to piss you off more than you are now. The second — well, let's just say that I'm not sure I'll want any kids. I have to go to the local school after this. He asked her if the school had known about the abuse. *Not only did they know about it, but also that he'd not been eating well. Something about not being able to talk to the parents. I don't know what their policy is on such things, but you can bet they know mine right now.*

Honey, I don't know if you're aware of this or not, but everyone knows what you're thinking because you have no trouble putting it out there. She thanked him. *You're welcome. And what is the second bit of news? So far, so you know, I don't know if this was the really bad or the really-really bad news.*

The first one is the bad. I thought I'd start with that. The second is that I've been able to locate the aunt. She's one of two of Duncan's sisters, by the way. I did some looking into soon-to-be-dead Duncan's head, and found out enough information about them to know that he hated them both, so they must be nice. Elliot laughed. *The one is not able to come here and see about the boy, nor to make arrangements for her sister-in-law's funeral. She said that she thought her sister was*

18

dead. *I think Duncan has been playing them both against each other. I've given her the information to contact her. Also, all arrangements have been made, including sending the plane for her and help with her children. Her name is Julia Harney, and she said that she won't see her brother. She'll arrive here in a couple of days. So, the bad news — or perhaps good, if you want to take him for your own son — is that she's coming to see Cody, but she's not taking him in. Told me right off that she had four kids of her own and didn't need another mouth to feed. Not mean like — she just sounded as if she was overwhelmed with life and just can't take any more. Single mom and all, she's barely making it on her own.*

What happens to him if he's not taken in by family? Emerald told him she was looking to see if there was a grandmother or such, but she didn't hold out much hope of anyone taking him. *So, he's going to be a ward of the state. After all he's been through, now he'll have to be in the system. That fucking sucks.*

You could adopt him. He had actually thought about it, in an offhanded sort of way. *I'm sure that you won't have any trouble taking him in. And once he's there, it's just a matter of getting the right paperwork done and filed. And you know as well as I do, he's better off with a vampire than he would be some of the bloodsucking fucks that are out there waiting on someone else to abuse. And I'm referring to some of the foster care homes that, you know as well as I do, only make it worse for a kid.*

Yes. Over the years I've come to realize that there are few that can be counted on to do what they're supposed to with a child. But I'll look into having him come live with me. Even if it's only temporary for now. She told him where he was, that he was being examined by the hospital. *He's not hurting as much as he was. And he's had a few healthy meals in him, so that'll be good for him as well.*

It's going to make a big difference to a lot of people, this kid being safe, and his fucktard of a dad put away. By the way, have you thought about your mate? He asked her what she meant. *I don't know, but it's been my experience that a mate will come out of nowhere for you guys. What if this woman with her children is the one for you?*

She was still laughing when he closed the connection. Some days he thought about strangling her. But he knew, just as soon as he was close enough to do something like that, he'd not have to worry about his brother hurting him. Emerald would hurt him in ways that he'd never thought of. No, he'd not hurt her, but he could think about it. Smiling for the first time since coming to this house, he felt better knowing that Cody was going to be safe for a while.

Chapter 2

Julia wasn't used to people being so nice to her. And to help her out with coming to see to Rose was something that she never thought would happen. Her kids were playing with brand new toys on the floor at her feet, and she was drinking the best glass of tea she'd ever had. She wondered if they were buttering her up to take Cody. She hoped not—they were going to be very disappointed if they were. She'd love to, but just could not afford it. She couldn't even afford to take care of her own properly.

There were days when she had to go without so that her kids could have food. And more days than not, she'd have to work on her homework well after they'd gone to bed so that she'd not think about how much she was fighting to keep her head level with the storm of things drowning her. But with the water that seemed to be getting deeper every day, it was a challenge on her part to keep them all happy and well fed. All in an effort to try and make something of herself.

She wanted to be a nurse in the worst kind of way. She figured that she would be able to mend her children when they got hurt, but most of all, she'd have a nice steady income. Money for a good babysitter for the kids, and most importantly, to put food in their bellies as well as her own.

"Mom, when we get to the hotel, do you think they'd mind if we took this stuff with us? We won't break it or nothing, I promise." She wanted to cry. Nodding at her oldest, she told him that she'd ask them. "Thanks, Mom. I think these people have a lot of money, don't you?"

She had four children, but only one of them was hers. When dickhead, as she'd started calling her ex-husband, had left her, he didn't take his own kids with him. Not that she minded having them in her life. But having five mouths to feed, including herself, and no income was harder than anyone could believe. He refused to send her any kind of support either. He told her she'd have to deal with it—he'd had to. Whatever that had meant.

Her son, Brett, was going to be nine in a couple of weeks. She'd scrimped and saved all she could to afford not just a small gift, but to make him a cake too. Luxuries like cake were well appreciated at the Henry home. And while the gift was cheap and made of plastic, she knew that like all the kids, he'd treasure it. They were all good kids, and she loved them very much.

When the very beautiful and polite woman that had been there on the private plane told them they'd be landing soon, she told the kids to get into their seats. Hayley, the youngest, took the small teddy bear from the toys and held it as they landed. Julia hoped that she'd be able to convince them to let her have

22

the little thing. Hayley had been so quiet holding onto him. Julia prayed that she wouldn't have to explain to the little girl that she wouldn't be able to keep the teddy bear if they said no. Nor to the other children about the gifts. Not that she expected them to just hand them over, but it had been thoughtful of them to provide them with some entertainment. For now, she'd let her play with it.

Julia hated being broke like this. And all because dickhead had decided that he liked fucking the woman that worked for him rather than helping out his real family. And even though he should have to pay her child support as well as something for rent and such, he'd never done a damned thing. And Julia had filed for divorce, but it seemed that dickhead had decided to wait until the very last moment to sign the papers and put the paperwork on file. She wished every day that she'd not met the bastard.

The plane came to a very smooth stop after the first bump of the landing. Gathering the kids up, she was ready to leave. But Alice, the stewardess, told her that she'd make sure that the toys were taken to the place they were staying.

Julia was so grateful that she started to cry. Feeling foolish to have been so emotional, she told Alice how sorry she was.

"No worries, Ms. Henry. I've been made aware of your situation. And I have to tell you, I'm so impressed with you. Not many would take on someone else's children, go to college to make themselves a better person, and have the politest wonderful children I've ever met."

She wasn't sure how she felt about someone knowing her situation, but she did appreciate the compliment. She had to figure that people with the kind of money that these people seemed to have, they'd not send a jet for a bad person. Getting into the long limo that was waiting for them on the tarmac, she told the children about the toys they'd been playing with.

"They're ours? Oh, I'm so happy." Shelby was eight and was very dramatic when she wanted to be. But no less adorable for it. "When I grow up, I want to be a stewardess. She has the prettiest clothes, don't you think, Mom?"

They all called her Mom—even Hayley, who couldn't have remembered her own mother. She told them they were very lucky, but they were to be on their best behavior. They didn't want to get stuck someplace without a ride home.

The house, not the hotel that she was thinking they'd be at, was as grand as any house she'd ever seen. Getting out, she saw the beautiful couple on the front porch. Then several more people came out of the house and stood there like they were waiting for something. Nate and Hayley hid behind her, but Brett stood in front of her with his fist doubled up and a look on his face that said no touching when the couple who had come out first walked toward them. The woman looked to be about four months pregnant. And happy.

"It's all right, Brett. I'm sure that they're not going to bring us all this way and hurt us now." He didn't move, not even when the beautiful woman got down on her knees in front of him. "This is my son, Brett. My other children are Nate, Shelby, and Hayley. They're a little protective of me."

"As they should be toward their mom. My name is Jewel Crosby. My husband is the man there, the one leaning against the car. His name is Jason. He would never harm any one of you, I promise." Jewel shook his hand and told Brett that she was sorry. "You're a brave and strong young man. I'm glad to see that you are the protector of your mom in all this."

Julia looked at Jewel's husband when he straightened up and stood. Christ, he was tall.

"Welcome to our home, Ms. Henry. And don't be sorry about your son's protectiveness. We're glad to see that you've someone in your corner. I think it's been a rough life for you and the kids." She nodded, overwhelmed at how nice they were being. "We've decided that it would more than likely be easier on you to stay at our home. It'll be hard enough on you without having the extra stress of watching out for the children. There are so many hands here wanting to hold and hug them, I don't think you have a thing to worry about while you're here. Come on, let me introduce you to my family."

Nodding again, she told them that she appreciated them helping her get here. And when Hayley allowed one of the other men to pick her up, Julia stopped walking and stared at her. When Jewel asked her if she was all right, she told her that Hayley never let anyone hold her but her.

"It's because she knows that she's safe here." Julia asked her if they were. "Oh yes, you are very safe. And we're here for you should you need us. You have nothing to worry about, I promise you. I did want to tell you that Cody is with my brother-in-law this morning. They've been working at cleaning up the greenhouse that was slightly damaged when Duncan was arrested."

"He's not a nice man. I know that he's my brother, but I'd just as soon not have anything to do with him. I'll make the arrangements for Rose's funeral as best I can, but that's all we can do while here. And if they don't allow me to make payments on it—well, I'm not sure I could even afford those right now. I'm sure that you've looked into our life." Jewel said that they had but she understood, and for some reason, Julia didn't think she was taking her all that seriously. "I have to go back when we're done here. I've taken up enough of your time. And if Dick.... I mean Nathan, discovers I've taken the children out of state, he'll...."

She never told anyone what sort of person she'd married. Julia closed her mouth on what she'd been about to tell this woman when she thought she might know. It made her a little mad, but she knew there was little she could do about it. Going into the house with the rest of the family, she thought that she'd have to watch what she said from now on.

They were shown to their rooms and she was overwhelmed again. They each had one of their own, and in the rooms were toys and other things that they could entertain themselves with. Brett had a computer in his room that one of the other men, Grayson, told him that he could watch movies or play games on. Nate and Shelby each had one in theirs as well. Taking Hayley to her room, which had an adjoining door to hers, Julia could see that it had been set up for a little girl.

Books were on the shelves, as well as a dollhouse with wooden furniture. There was a tablet that Jewel had told her was programmed with parental controls. Pulling the woman aside, she had to tell her that this was too much, and that they were going to be disappointed when they left.

"We're hoping that you'll stay here. It'll give you and the children a fresh start. You won't have to worry about Duncan coming into your life again. With this family, we protect those that mean something to us. And you have wormed your way into our hearts already." Julia asked her why they'd even think that. "We'll talk at dinner. I'm not trying to fob you off or anything, but I need to go back to the plant, and the rest of the family is out working too. We're working today so we can have the rest of the week off with you and your family."

When she was gone, Julia looked around. What was she supposed to do with all this wealth? Not that any of it was hers, but it was a lot to take in for someone that hadn't had the money for even the simplest things. And what would she tell her children when they had to go back to their two-bedroom home with nothing in the way of toys or books that they could use?

Going to the bed, she wasn't surprised to see Hayley there sleeping. It had been a stressful few days for her too. Lying on the bed after telling the other children not to make any noise and not to leave their rooms, she laid down too. Her head was spinning from all this. No one was that generous to a stranger. Closing her eyes, she meant only to rest but fell asleep almost as soon as the soft comforter touched her cheek. Her last thought was, she really did feel safe here.

Disoriented when she woke up, Julia had a moment of fear. Her children. Dashing from room to room, she saw that they were all gone, and so was Hayley. Running down the stairs, ready to do battle for them, Julia heard them in the room ahead of her. Going there, she stopped in her tracks when she saw two men, obviously related to Chase, making sandwiches for her children and talking to them. She didn't have a clue what the topic was, but it was nice hearing them so excited about something. And the laughter spilling from their lips.

"You should have seen him. He came running out of the barn like his butt was on fire. I swear to you, I've never laughed so hard in my life." The kids laughed, and Julia felt a smile tug at her mouth. "And to this day, he not only won't go in the barn, but he stays away from the cows there too."

They were safe. Not only that, but they were relaxed too, not hiding in fear that someone would harm them. Going into the kitchen the rest of the way, she smiled at the two men there and asked if the kids had been any trouble.

"On the contrary, they've been very well behaved. And we've had fun, haven't we?" The kids all nodded as they were eating thick ham sandwiches with potato chips. "I'm Ryan, and that's my younger brother, Sean. We're brothers to Chase."

"My goodness, there must be a lot of you guys." Sean told her that there were six boys, as his dad called them. And two sisters-in-law, as well as their dad and new stepmom. "I think your dad needs to have a look at you guys. You're no more boys than I am."

"Yes, well, it's hard to have him break a habit. How did you sleep? You must have needed it." She said that she felt better. "Emerald, one of our sisters-in-law, said that she'd be by later to take you to the funeral home. She drives like she cusses, just so you know. And no matter how much we've told her to be nice around the kids, I wouldn't expect too much with her. She's set in her ways too."

Nodding, Julia wondered what they'd say if they knew that her kids had heard it all when dickhead came around. But she didn't. Taking the glass of tea when it was handed to her, she was fixed a sandwich too. These men knew how to treat a lady, she thought.

The door opened behind her and she turned to look at yet another clone of the three Crosbys that she'd met so far. He looked stronger than the two in the room with her, and she had a feeling that he wasn't one to mess with. There was something about him that made her think of him slaying dragons for them. When he was hugged, and tightly, by the other men, she wondered what it would be like to be loved that much.

"Hello." Nodding, she stayed in her seat, afraid that she'd make a fool of herself once again. Since coming here she'd been a blubbing fool. Then the door opened again and there was Cody. He ran to her arms when she said his name, and she cried anyway.

~~~

Elliot stood away from the woman. He couldn't smell anything different about her but that she seemed to be terribly tense and terrified. That did put out an overwhelming scent that had his beast beating at him to take care of her. Every time someone got too close to her or the children, she'd stiffen. There wasn't any way he was going to try and see if she was his mate when she was as skittish as a newborn kitten.

Cody had been that way at first too. Wounded animal was all he could think about. The family was like a bunch of people that had gone through hell, and while they had survived, it had cost them all.

Emerald came into the room just as he was making himself a sandwich. Elliot thought that this might be fun to watch.

"You have a house. Go there and leave some for the rest of us. You would not believe the fucking idiot that I had to deal with today. I swear, men only think with one thing, and it's not the brains in their heads." Ryan cleared his throat and Emerald flipped him off. "I'm sure that they've heard all this before. And I'm betting that they know more curse words than I do.

Don't they?"

Elliot asked her if there was any way that she'd tone it down when Emerald sat at the table with the kids and Julia. When she started talking to them, he could hear the different tone in her voice, and wondered if she had any idea that she'd toned it down anyway.

"I need to tell you all something. And it's important that you listen to me in this, all right?" They each nodded at her, and Elliot wondered what was going on that would have Emerald of all people having a conversation with kids. "Your uncle is out of jail. I'm not sure what has happened there, something about the fucking police not doing their job, but I don't want you to go outside by yourself. He's dangerous."

Cody came to stand next to Elliot and took his hand. The kid had been in such a good mood to see his cousins, and now this. He tightened his grip on his hand and told him it would be all right. But he was to listen to Emerald.

"He's got out, and he killed my mom." Elliot told him that he'd be safe. "I know you keep telling me that, but he's going to be really mad when he comes here again. And what if you get hurt? What am I gonna do then?"

"You'll be safe. I promise you. Have I lied to you about that so far?" Cody said that he'd not. "I told you that we'd tell you the truth all the time, didn't I? And you have to believe me when I tell you you're going to be safe—all of you will be."

"Yes, sir."

Elliot looked at the others who were staring at him and Cody. When Cody started to cry again, they each got up and patted him on the back. Children, Elliot thought, were much better at comforting each other than adults could be.

When Emerald sent them off to play, Cody went with them. Elliot was glad for it. When they moved to the dining room, they sat there talking about not much of anything, waiting for the rest of the family to show up. He glanced at Julia. She looked ready to bolt. He decided that now, before she was overwhelmed too much more, he needed to find out what, if anything, she was to him.

"I'd like to explain things to you, if you'll be all right with a little more news." She looked at him, and he wanted to comfort her in the worst kind of way. "We're not human. None of us are. And you'll meet the rest of us in a little while."

"Not human. I should have guessed that." He asked her why. "Wealthy beyond anything that I've ever seen. Good looking, with women that are just as beautiful as you're all handsome. Strong too, like you've been lifting weights for a hundred years. So, what are you? Something that is going to scare the crap out of me too?"

"I hope not, but I don't know. We're vampires." She stood up and sat down twice before he realized that she was going to stay there this time. "We're not going to hurt you."

"Yes, well, humans have been telling me that shit for a long time now. And look where it's gotten me. Not that I don't love those children in the other room, but I've not been able to provide for them like I should. Not to mention, how I'd love to." He nodded and told her he was sorry. "For what? Being rich? I'm sure that you've worked really hard for it. And so you know, you wear it well. Are you sorry that I won the lottery in having a shitty life? That's not your fault either. I'm the one that married him. But I honestly don't think there is too much more that can shock me. I've about hit the limit for that, I think."

31

"I'm afraid that things aren't going to be any better for you right now. I was informed on the way here that your ex has found out that you've left town and is currently trying his best to find out where you are." Elliot watched her face and knew the exact moment that she realized how much trouble she really was in. Elliot didn't have any idea how to help her in her breakdown. As surely as he was sitting there with her, he knew that she was going to have one. But she seemed to stiffen up, like she was trying her best to make them all think that she was made of stronger stuff.

"When I married him, I had no idea that he had kids. Not that I don't love them, but I didn't know. He knew about Brett—I was honest in telling him. But he wasn't the same for me." Elliot asked her when he started abusing her. "Just after he brought his kids to live with us. About a week after. When I asked him, quite innocently, if they were going back with their mother, he hit me so badly that I had to go to the hospital. After that, it was as if I became his punching bag. I figured it was better for him to hit me than one of them. And he hated Brett with a passion. I suppose because he's not his. Then one day, about four years after we were married, he not only moved out but told me he wasn't returning. When I asked him why, he told me that it was too much work being a dad to so many kids, and that he was leaving them with me. There were prettier and sexier women out that there that didn't have a bunch of brats. I've often wondered if he realized that I only had brats, as he called them, because they were mostly his."

"Did he do that legally? Leave you with the kids, I mean?" She said that it was in the divorce papers. She'd gotten full custody of the kids—she'd made sure of that when he told her

32

that he didn't want them. "I take it that didn't matter to him. He held them over your head a great deal."

"Yes, well, he knew just what strings to pull." She looked at him then and he let her. He didn't bother trying to hide what he was from her. If she was his mate, then she'd have to know anyway. "Why are you all being so nice to me? You don't have to be. You could have let Cody go into the system and no one would have cared. The little guy was in no better shape than we are and would more than likely do better in a home with someone else."

"I doubt he would have felt like I'd done him a favor. Besides, I like him. When I first found him staying in my greenhouse, my first instinct was to call someone. I didn't want him to be hurt, and I thought he might have been a runaway or something. Even kids with the best of homes do that." She nodded. "Anyway, being what I am, I was able to not only tell that he was terrified out of his mind, but that he was also abused. And bad enough that he could barely move when necessary."

"Emerald, she said that Duncan was out. That he'd gotten free because of something that the police had done. Do you know that for sure? Or did he pay them off? If there is one thing I know about my brother, he will do anything to keep from going to jail." Elliot asked her if he had money to do something like that. "Yes. So does my ex. But they don't want to spend it on their families. It would mean that they'd have to share. And neither of them were good at sharing."

It was time, he thought, to figure this thing out with her. Elliot told her what he needed to do, to rule out whether or not she was his mate. Before he could lean into her throat, he looked up at Jason when he came into the room. There was something wrong.

Instead of going to him to find out what was happening, he pulled Julia closer to him and inhaled deeply. She smelled good, like fresh flowers in the spring, but she wasn't his mate. Standing up to go with Jason, he had never felt so disappointed in his life than he was at that moment.

She wasn't his mate. Those children would never be his for him to protect and help raise. Of course, he could and would help her when she'd let him, but he was profoundly disappointed.

"There's some trouble at Crosby's Flowers. The police are already there, and they were afraid that you were there too. Thankfully you have all those faeries working with you, or it might have been a total loss." They got into his truck to go see what had happened. "She's not your mate."

"No, and you have no idea how I feel about that. I've fallen in love with young Cody. And those other kids, they're wonderful. But Julia isn't mine, and I'm so depressed about that." Jason told him he was sorry. "So am I. I guess she's out there, but this was a blow to my heart for reasons I don't even understand."

As soon as they got out of the truck, he could see that the damage wasn't as bad as his mind had made it out to be. He expected it to be ash, but there was only a little destruction to the front where he was going to have the cash register set up. The fire department came to him as soon as he shook hands with Joe.

"I can tell that it was Duncan. He's got it out for you. And if I can prove it was him, he'll be back in jail in no time." Elliot asked him if this was the only damage. "Yes. Lucky for you that there is live in help for you. Otherwise, I'm not sure we would have been able to save any of it."

The faeries and brownies had taken over the greenhouse in the last few months. It was warmer in there, of course, but the added bonus for them was that there was a place for them to plant seeds year-round. He saw them as soon as he walked into the building. One of them landed on his shoulder as he looked around.

"If you were to give us permission to take care of the man, we shan't have this trouble again." He told James, the little brownie, that he had to be dealt with by the justice system even though he'd like him gone as well. "Well then, if he comes back, we'll handle it so that he lives, but he'll know that we mean business. I doubt that he will return anyway. He was given quite the scare when we came out of the building as smoke was billowing up around our ears."

"Good. I'll start having some of the pack that roams my land come by once in a while so that they can keep you safe as well." He said that he was sorry about the building. "The building can be replaced, you cannot. Just stay safe for me and things will work themselves out."

"Yes, my lord." He moved through the building, looking at the damage that had been done. James told him of the few things that he'd noticed as well, and told him that the faeries could fix that, no problem. "I'm going to set them on the water lines too. You had them working, but they think they can improve on it. You've done a good job for them, sir; they wish only to repay you."

"They mean the world to me. And I need a favor. Would you send someone to help out Ms. Henry? Not just help her, but keep an eye on the children as well. I believe that we're setting her up in a home if she'll agree to stay here. I have no reason to believe that she won't, but I won't make assumptions for anyone." He said that he'd send some to meet her today. "Be careful how you go to her, James. She's had a very rough time of it, and it will stress her out more to have a scare like all of us might be to her."

It took him about an hour to assess the damage. It really wasn't much, and it would be fixed before he could get a check from the insurance company. Elliot didn't bother going back to his brother's house afterwards. Stress was taking him under lately.

Chapter 3

The phone was ringing when she got into her apartment. It had been a day from hell, and Hannah didn't think she could take much more without a long nap, a weeks' worth, as well as a better job. Not that the one she had didn't pay well, but she traveled too much and worked overtime without being paid for it. She hated her boss but loved what she did as a researcher.

She answered the phone too harshly, she knew, but she wasn't going to explain herself if this was some robot call or a telemarketer. They were forever taking up her time, and she was going to report them. To whom, she had no idea, but she despised them.

"Hannah Kline?" She said it was and asked who the hell she was. "Oh, I think I like you. Very much. I'm Emerald Crosby. I'm calling on behalf of your sister, Julia. She's having a rough time of it."

"Aren't we all?" Laying her head against the cabinet in front of her, Hannah let out a long breath. "I've had a really shitty day and I don't anticipate it getting any better. I do have a sister named Julia, but he told me that she was dead. Or was to me, I don't remember now. But she married that fucking idiot Nathan and he cut me off from seeing her. I didn't even know that she's alive until this minute. So, I don't know what's happened to her if you're looking for her."

"She's divorced dickhead, what she calls him. Or rather, he's left her high and dry for what he thinks of as a better, sexier piece of ass. The idiot, which is a perfect name for him, as well as dickhead, is looking for her as we speak. His sister, Rose, was murdered a few weeks back by her own husband." Hannah laughed, but it was bitter and painful. "Julia also thought that you were dead."

"I figured as much. Nathan couldn't stand that we were close at one time. And I tried very hard to convince her not to marry the piece of shit. Where is she now?" The woman told her. "I'm sorry, but I'm in no better shape than she is at the moment. I have the nicest job you could imagine, but the boss is a bigger prick than our dad used to be to our mom when we were kids. I just got home from traveling around the country, and my boss wants me to come in tonight and tell him all about what happened. In detail, mind you. I need to either go in or he'll bring his happy ass to me. And I don't feel like being chased around my couch, thanks."

"I've already sent someone to come for you." She asked her why she'd do something like that. "You'll see that we're a family of very protective beings, and I think that with you here, she'll feel better about staying nearby so we can protect her. Not to mention being safer with us. We, my family and I, have taken her kids into our hearts."

"Kids? She has more than Brett?" Emerald told her what had happened. "That fucking son of a bitch. You know, his parents would have had a better kid had they just let that shit hit the sheets instead of making a thing like him."

Emerald laughed, and Hannah felt a smile tug at her own lips. It was good to hear someone think she had a sense of humor. Even to have one made her feel almost human again. And she thought perhaps the woman was right, they would be good friends. Under different circumstances. Emerald was saying the same thing and again, Hannah smiled.

"Yes, I think we're going to be good friends, like I said. Anyway, the man I sent for you is Elliot Crosby, my brother-in-law. He's going to show you his driver's license before you allow him in. Dickhead is on his way as well, thinking that you have his wayward ex-wife." Hannah said she thought that she could handle Nathan. "Perhaps. But if your sister finds out that you're alive and that he's after you, she'll come to you. And that would be bad for all of you."

"And what do you think I can do for her? I'm not as broke as I'm sure she is, but I don't have much. I might even lose my job after today. It would be a good thing for me, not so much for the company I work for." Emerald asked her what she did. "I'm an assistant to this shithead, not much different than dickhead is. But he doesn't know his ass from a hole in the ground, and he certainly doesn't know how to do his job. I'm a researcher and I'm damned good at what I do. If I do say so myself."

"Well, then he'll be shit out of luck. Maybe coming out here for your sister might be the best thing that happens to him. He might be able to get his head out of his ass and figure out a good thing when he had it." Hannah told her that she doubted it. "Yeah, me too. But you'll come out, right?"

"Sure, why the fuck not? Just don't expect too much from me. I'm more of a kick your ass type of person than one to try and be nice about shit." Emerald laughed, and Hannah had the urge to smile again. She might like this person as well. "You and I, we're going to bump heads a great deal, aren't we?"

"Oh, I'm sure of it. And, so you know, everyone is afraid of me here. It'll be kind of fun having someone just like me to talk to." Hannah didn't comment but did ask her when Elliot was coming out to get her. "He's more than likely pretty close to you now. Let me find out."

She wasn't put on hold as she thought she might have been. Hannah could hear voices in the background. A man asking about dinner, another talking about the businesses that he was working with. Hannah pulled her dinner from last night out of the fridge and wondered if she could reheat something four days in a row. When the doorbell rang, she made her way to it, holding the phone.

"That would be my brother-in-law. He said to tell you that you're not safe in the place where you're living, and you should move out." She told Emerald that if he was going to pass judgment on her living arrangements, wait until he saw her car. "Yes, well, he also said to tell you that he needs to be invited in."

Hannah was just opening the door when what Emerald said occurred to her. The man standing on the other side of her doorway didn't move, but he did smile at her. The fangs—all she could see was the fact that he had fangs.

"Vampire." He nodded and then looked in the direction she was. "I don't want to be accused of stating the obvious, but it's daytime. I mean, like the hottest part of the day, daytime."

"I've been given a great gift of being able to be out in the sun like a human." She asked him when he'd fed last. "You're very informed. But recently. Are you going to invite me in? Your neighbors are watching us through their peepholes."

"I'm not sure yet. But we're going to set come ground rules." He nodded. "I'm not a snack or a meal for you or anyone in your family, got it?"

"Yes, and so you know, we've never been the type of vampires that take without permission. Much less from friends." She nodded. "I don't need to come into your home if you can pack up and come with me soon. As I said, we're being watched."

"I read once, a long time ago, that I can put stipulations on inviting you in. That I can say that you can come in this one time, but not again without permission again." He smiled and told her that was right. "All right, you can come in this one time, but no other time without my permission."

"You forgot something." She cocked her head at him and asked him what it was. "You can bar me from tasting you as well. Or anyone that comes into your home that you'd rather didn't. That rule applies to all kinds of shifters, including wolves and cats."

"All right. You may come into my home this one time, but you're not to taste any part of me." She stepped back when he came into the room. "Christ, I thought you were big out there, but in here you're absolutely ginormous, aren't you?"

"Emerald said I was to tell you that Nathan is in town and that he has your address. That if you're going to be safe from him, we need to go now." Nodding, Hannah looked around.

"Your home is very stark, isn't it?"

"I grew up with nothing and I've never had anything since." She turned to him when she picked up her backpack, what she carried instead of a purse. "If you're ready to go, so am I. I want to see my sister and get her situated, then come back here. I think I quit my job today, or I got fired—I'm not sure which—but if he needs me, he knows how to find me. My boss, I mean."

They were going down the stairs when he stopped her suddenly and pulled her behind him. Hannah was too startled by the move to say anything. Then she saw Nathan.

He'd gotten fat over the years. And his hair, usually so neat and clean, was messy and seemed to be thinning a great deal. As he walked by them, she could see the gun in his pocket, the outline of a knife that was in his back pocket too. Holding onto Elliot as he held her in place, Hannah closed her eyes against the overwhelming fear that seemed to wash over her.

"He will not harm you." Elliot was standing in front of her, facing her this time. "Breathe. You need to inhale and exhale for me. Come on. If I have to carry you out of here, people are going to wonder why. And I'd just as soon not get arrested today."

She did as he told her, watching his face as he breathed with her. Hannah didn't scare easily, nor was she a faint of heart type of person. But suddenly, here and now, she was afraid for her life. And she knew that it had very little to do with the vampire in front of her. Nathan had always hated her and she him. But he was violent with his hatred, while she was just mouthy.

"Are you okay now?" She nodded. "Good. I have you. You don't have to worry about him finding you. Nor harming you. All right?"

"Yes, all right. He was coming here to hurt me, wasn't he? Not hurt—no, he would have killed me for answers that I don't have." Elliot nodded and kept watching her. "I'm all right now. Let's go."

"There is something else that you should know before we go much further." She looked at him, almost afraid of what might come out of his mouth. "You're my mate. I wanted you to know that before we got home."

She was dragged more than helped along the way. The ride to the airport was done in a haze for her. Mate. That was all that kept going through her mind. She was the mate to a fucking huge vampire.

When they were on the plane, a private one no less, he sat her down on the seat and buckled her in. Hannah grabbed his hair when he leaned over her to snap the belt closed.

"I'm not easy. Nor am I going to fall into bed with you just because you think you can make me with your magical eyes." He winked at her. "I don't charm well either, nor are you to think that just because you've told me this, I'm going to believe you. I'm not stupid at all, and if you think so, you're in for a rude awakening, buster."

"This is something that I'd never lie to you about. In fact, you should know that I cannot lie to you. Not that I would, but I can't even if I wanted to." She nodded but didn't let go of his hair yet. "Anything else bothering you at this moment?"

"Yes, but for now, I can't think past the fact that Nathan came to my home with the intent of harming me." He told her that he would have killed her had he not been able to help her. "Is this part of the honesty thing? If it is, for now, just don't answer me on shit like this. I need to cope, and that's not helping."

He was laughing as he leaned back in his own chair. Her hands were still warm from holding onto him, and she had to shake herself into not thinking about how wonderful he'd made her feel in those few moments. Hannah was well and truly over her head right now, and she had no idea why she felt that he'd help her.

She'd not been letting anyone into her life for a long time, not since her sister had just seemed to fall off the face of the earth. Nathan had done that too—taken Julia away from her so finally that she thought her little sister was dead. She asked Elliot how he'd become involved with this all.

He told her the whole sordid story, and she wondered why people with children couldn't just make it easier on them for once. Poor Cody and the rest of the kids. To be related to such families was almost like having her own parents alive. Life, she had come to realize, had a way of coming full circle. Looking at Elliot, she wondered what sort of demands he'd put on her before she had to stake him. And she would if he fucked with her.

~~~

Elliot didn't tell anyone that Hannah was his mate. He supposed that he should have told someone, but he was still trying to wrap his mind around it himself. A mate was something that he'd sort of been looking forward to, but he had hoped that it would be a normal quiet relationship, not one filled with murder and intrigue. But then, he supposed that this was reality and not a dream.

You all right, son? He told his dad that he was fine, just thinking. *Thinking pretty hard too, if you ask me. Anything I can help you work out?*

I found her, Dad. My mate, and she's a ball buster like Emerald. His dad laughed and told him congratulations. *She's very outspoken and makes me want to pull her into my arms and hold her until she likes me.*

I'm sure that she does like you. Elliot didn't bother saying anything to his dad, but waited for him to speak again. *You and the other boys, you sure have done this man proud in bringing home women that a man could be happy with. Even though some of them scare me, I'm happy that they're in our lives.*

Her name is Hannah, Hannah Kline. And she's this beautiful creature that makes me laugh. Even though the timing is off, I still want to laugh. She also has a good bit of knowledge of our kind. He told him what she'd said about inviting him in. *I guess she might have had contact with a couple of vampires in her lifetime. Or she might have done some research on us. That's what she does for a living, a researcher of some repute.*

I would guess, son, that she might have known a few vampires, but it's doubtful that she has had any contact with anyone like us. He told his dad that was true. *You should talk to her about it while you're in the sky. It's doubtful that she'd throw you from the plane, but I'd keep an eye on her should you upset her.*

He told his dad that he would and glanced at Hannah. She was looking around the cabin of the plane they were in, and he wondered what was in her head. He could have peeked, but that would be lying or something close to it. Instead, he started telling her about himself.

"I have a home. It's a good sized one and something that I've owned for a while, but if you don't care for it, we can search for something else." Hannah looked at him then. "But I want to start at the beginning, so that you can know me a little better. Of what I have to tell you, anyway. Like me, you'll be learning things that come to us aren't quite the norm either. A faerie queen, Kilian is her name, needed us. There was a fire that someone had set, and we, my brothers, father, and I, helped her get out of it. Her and a great many of her faeries."

"A fire? How long ago was this?" He stopped to think about it and she laughed. "If you have to think on it that hard, I can assume that it was a very long time ago."

"Yes, hundreds and hundreds of years, as a matter of fact. But back to my story so that you have a better understanding of us all. The reason that I could come and see you during the day, Kilian gave us a gift when we saved her, the gift of sunlight." She nodded and looked at him as he continued. "Over the centuries, my family and I worked hard to become a part of the human race. It was difficult, as you can well imagine, but the ability to be out in the sun helped us blend in better than most could have. It also, more than likely, saved our lives a few times."

"That first time you saw the sun, how was it for all of you? I'm imagining you lying about, letting your tender skin get burnt and loving every minute of it." He laughed and told her that they had gotten burnt, but because they had thought it was only for the one day, they had wanted to soak up as much as they could. "I think that would have been the saddest thing in the world, to be given something great only to know that it would all be gone soon. Or thinking that, anyway."

"When we were able to go out in the sun after that, Kilian came to us to tell us what else she'd given us. And it was a great deal of magic to go along with the sunlight. We were better off than most humans, and tremendously better off than any vampires we knew." He looked at her face, knowing that so long as he lived, this was going to be a face he would love. "Jason met his wife, Jewel. You'll like her—she's the kindest, most wonderful person you could met. We all love her very much for taking him on and bringing him into this decade. He was sort of old fashioned in his ways, and that pissed her off. And that is an understatement if you want to know the truth. But they're fine now and going to have a baby soon."

He thought of how much Jason had gone through. and wondered if he regretted not being nicer from the start. Elliot was sure that he did. He knew that he would. Thinking about the things that had been happening to them all, he thought of Emerald.

"You've spoken to Emerald. On the phone." Hannah nodded and said she was something else. "You have no idea. She's not human either, but an ice dragon. Not an actual dragon, but the protector of them. Until recently that is. Now, her and my brother, Chase, are the king and queen of all dragons, and rule them. It's a pretty big deal. Emerald has these two tiny dragons that are with her at all times. But don't get it in your head that they're warm and cuddly. They're far from it. They'll kill, and without any thought to who it is. But only when Emerald tells them to."

"Don't piss off Emerald, check. But you make it sound as if I should be impressed." He told her that he wasn't, he was only telling her about his family. "I know, Elliot. I was joking you. And so you know, I am impressed. Dragons and queens and kings. Faerie and vampires. I knew about most of the other creatures in the world, but not all, apparently. Vampires and wolves for sure. A cat or two as well. But the rest? No, I had no idea."

"You'll learn to go with it after a while." He wondered briefly if he should tell her now that she was an immortal and decided that she needed it all. "Emerald gave us a part of herself, and in turn, our mates have that magic as well. We're true immortals. You are as well since the moment that we touched. I'm not entirely sure how it works but being my mate and me simply touching you gave you the power as well."

She looked around again and didn't speak. He didn't try and tell her more, Elliot knew that she was overwhelmed by all this already. He just let it sink into her mind, much as it had his own when he'd met her.

Hannah was beautiful. He supposed that he was slightly prejudiced about her looks because of what she was to him. His mate would be beautiful to him no matter what. He wanted to tell her that too, explain to her how much she already meant to him. But again, he was going slowly for her sake. Elliot wasn't sure now that he wanted to go directly home—he wanted Hannah all for himself.

"True immortal. What does that mean? And when you say that as your mate, I'd have it too, is that true or are you hoping to get laid?" He told her that it was true, then explained to her what a true immortal was. "No, say I got really pissed off at you and decided that I'd had enough of your shit. I couldn't kill you by staking you?"

"No, and I'd hope that you'd talk to me first before trying to do that." She nodded, but he wasn't sure that she would at this point. "My head can't be removed either. Just in case you want to go that route."

She wasn't angry, but she did look at him. Elliot smiled at her, not hiding the fact that his beast was showing himself too. She didn't move away from him nor did she say anything. They just looked at one another like they were trying to memorize each part of them.

"People haven't been all that nice to me. Not to my sister either, for that matter. I've always thought that was why she married the idiot, because she thought that he was the best that she could do. I was never going to settle for anyone that didn't worship me. I know that's over the top, but I was only ten at the time, and I've since changed my mind about what I want."

"And what is it you want? A man that worships you? I'm that man. I know that you find that hard to believe right now, but it's the truth. I'll forever put you first in my life, even over myself. Do you want a man that will give you whatever you wish? I have a feeling that would bore you to tears, but I'd be willing to give you that." She asked him why he'd say such a thing. "It's the truth. I will never lie to you, as I said. I won't hurt you in any way if I can help it. I'm old, very old, and set in my ways for some things. But for you, for the rest of my life, I'd change myself to make you happy."

"I don't understand any of this." He nodded, and Elliot told her that he didn't either. She was his mate and they'd learn things together. "I have to think about all of this. I'm not sure what I do or don't believe. I'm too overwhelmed now to even think that any of this is real."

He was saved from telling her that it was about as real as it got when it was announced that they would be landing soon. Elliot didn't have any idea what he might have said to her if he'd continued telling her about himself. He was sure that she'd

49

not want to hear that he'd fallen in love with her the moment that she opened her door to him.

They landed about thirty minutes later, both of them not speaking again. He could tell that her mind was working, and as tempting as it was to see how she felt about him, he stayed out of her thoughts. As they were disembarking, he wondered if his dad had told the rest of them that Hannah was his mate, and that was cleared up as soon as they entered the little airport.

They were all there. Not just Hannah's sister, but the children as well. His dad held up a sign that welcomed her to Ohio, and he could see that he'd also written "to the family." But he was happiest to see how much Julia was glad to see her sister. Elliot could not imagine thinking that one of his brothers had died and then finding out that it had been a lie. They all hugged Hannah and him. You'd think that he'd been gone for years and not the couple of hours or so that he had been.

"We decided to come into town, meet the new family member, and have some dinner as a big old happy family." He hugged his dad for thinking of this. "Also, we're going to update the young lady here on things that are going on. It's not a mess so much as it is confusing. But that man, he's been making it his business to get on my last remaining nerve as far as he's concerned. And you know how hard I've been watching my temper." They all knew that and were proud of him for it.

"What has he done now?" Dad told him that they'd eat first, then talk. He had no plans of having indigestion over this man. "All right. I can live with that. But so you know, I'm going slowly with Hannah. Just to make her trust me."

"That's a good idea, son. Never run in where fools have gone, or something like that." He hugged his dad again and felt a small hand curl into his. He looked over at Cody and told him that he'd missed him too. "And that boy there, I think you should adopt him. He'd be a good grandson for this old man."

"You were never old, Dad." He watched as Hannah and her sister talked. "She's had a rough life. I'm going to make it my business to make sure that the rest of it is much better."

"You always were the smart one." Elliot had heard his dad say that to each of them over the years. "Oh, by the way, I've had a crew go in and do a dusting of your house. I noticed the last time I was there you had a lot of the rooms closed off. You could use some furniture too, I think."

"I was actually thinking about the warehouse that we own. There are a lot of things in that place that I can use." Dad asked if he'd take Hannah with him. "Yes, I'd like for her to pick out what she wants for our house. Why do you ask?"

"I was thinking about going with you if you don't mind. Maybe taking Brandy with me to have a look. We're looking into buying us a house too. And she wants to have children with me." He just stared at his dad, not sure what to say about that. "She's young and loves me. I haven't told her no or yes, but I did want to talk it over with you boys first. It'll mean you have a half-brother or sister."

"No, Dad, it'll mean we have another sibling. And while we tease you about calling us your boys, I think it would do you a world of good to have a child with Brandy. She'll make you feel like you've won the lottery." Dad said she did that already. "Good. And I would love for you to have me another brother or sister. Whenever you want."

Chapter 4

Duncan knew that his son was someplace in that house that was as big as a fucking hotel. But so far, he'd had no luck getting him when he came out of the thing. He also knew that the brat had been telling them everything he knew about him. Duncan no more liked that than he did the kid, but that wasn't any way to treat your own dad. He'd taken care of his wife blabbering about things that she shouldn't, and the kid was going to be next if the cops didn't stop fucking around with him. He looked at the mess in his house and wondered where he was going to find someone to clean it up. It was beginning to smell too.

He didn't necessarily want to kill shit for brains, but he did enjoy beating him up a bit. Really a lot of beatings. The kid was useful for things too. Like going to the store when he didn't want to. Getting the check out of the mailbox when Duncan had a splitting headache from too much beer the night before. He could also be counted on to clean up after him after his mom was taken care of. That had been a stroke of genius, him making Cody—he had forgotten his name until then—watch as he killed off his first bit of trouble. He'd been in line since then—until he ran off, anyways.

Rose hadn't been a bad wife. Not before Cody came along anyway. She'd allow him to beat on her until she was out cold and never say a word to anyone. Then after the kid was born, she'd changed into this wildcat where he was concerned. That kid had taken his place somehow, and he hated him for that. Duncan had tried his best to smother the ugly squalling baby, but again, Rose was right on top of that shit, and he didn't ever get the chance.

As soon as Cody had been old enough to go to school, Duncan had started taking care of Rose. The fucking bitch had been holding out on him and he wanted her to pay. And when she'd ask for shit for the kid, well, that just sent him into fits. It was Duncan's money that his mom and dad had left him, not for her to try and take. Not that she knew shit about that, but he wasn't giving her anything.

Duncan watched the cars go by the house. The cop cars didn't pull into the drive anymore, but that mattered little to him. This place wasn't really his, but the government's. Though there was another house where he hid out in when he could. It had his name on the deed, so he figured he could do as he damn well pleased with it. His mom had left it to him, unbeknownst to the government people, and he liked it that way. Besides, him not telling anybody that he owned it got Rose out and getting the food card. And a near free house for her to live in. He pretended to stay there with her and the kid, but the other place, it was his home—the one where he spent a lot of time lately. Ever since the cops had to let him go, and that stroke of luck was going to not just get him his kid, but some fun too. Couldn't arrest a man for the same crime twice. He'd seen that on a cop show once.

He needed some food in the house, he just realized. Looking for the card wasn't something that he wanted to do today, but he did look around. Duncan knew that the money showed up on the thing early in the month. He didn't know the date, not really, but food would suddenly appear in the house around then and that's what he'd surmised. She could cook a mean pot roast, he suddenly remembered.

There was blood on everything. By now he'd thought that he'd have his kid back so that he could get this cleaned up. What good was having a brat if not for picking up after you? But in order to get his shit together, Duncan knew that he was going to have to clean up the mess himself. At least enough where it wasn't all over the kitchen where he had to eat.

The knock at his front door had him looking around for his gun. He'd forgotten that it had been taken with a great many other things in his house when he'd been illegally arrested. This shit was for the birds. And if that fucker at the front door was the cops again, he was going to be highly pissed and not responsible for what he did to them. They were trespassing sure as shit.

The man standing there looked familiar. Where he'd seen him before, Duncan didn't have a clue. As soon as the man smiled and walked right in like he owned the place, Duncan wanted to kill him. The amount of rage he had in that second nearly consumed him. But the man started talking.

"You're married...well, you were married to my sister, Rose. I'm Nathan Henry. You and I have a lot in common, I think. We both want to kill someone *special* in our lives." Duncan didn't admit to anything. For all he knew this guy could be working with the cops. "I'm here to strike up a deal with you, and I think we can both be happy."

"I don't know you from anybody." Nathan walked over to the wall where Rose had crammed a lot of pictures and took down the one of them being married. He showed him who he was in the picture. "So? If you're looking for Rose, you'll be disappointed. She's dead."

"I know. And thank you for that. She was a pain in my ass for a while now. Our parents wanted us to split all the money that they left to us when they died. She kept on harping on me to give her the share that was coming to her. The attorneys, the fucking dicks, said I had to give her her part of it, and it was sent to her weeks ago. I think she planned on leaving you with it. You still have it?" Duncan hadn't seen any money and was positive that she'd been holding out on him with that too. He told Nathan what he was thinking. "That figures. Women are the ruination of the world. If it wasn't for pussy, then I'd have nothing to do with them. And kids. Do you have any?"

"One, but he's taken off from me and I'm having a hard time figuring out where he is." He told him he had six kids. "You're a better man than me. I couldn't stand the one we had, much less six of them."

"Julia, my ex-soon-to-be-dead wife, your stupid sister, has three of mine with her now. She's so stupid that she took on my kids like they were her own. She's dumber than a post if you ask me. But I guess you'd know that. And I have two bastards that I don't have shit to do with. And one with this girlfriend that I have now. I told her not to get knocked up and look what she went and done. I can't stand kids."

Duncan thought that if he hated them as much as this man was saying, he might have done something about it himself. There was no point in counting on the woman to be careful. They'd lie to you like it was their job if they thought they could get a nickel out of you. He sat down on one of the chairs in the kitchen when Nathan did and was glad that he hadn't wiped the blood off it before joining him in the other chair.

"What is your plan? If you want me to kill my sister for you, I must tell you that the cops are on my tail right now as if they're wanting to ride it like a broom handle. I just want my kid back so that I can get him to clean up this mess and cook for me. My sisters, they'd tell on me in a heartbeat if they thought it would get me into trouble. Of course, I do plan on knocking him around a bit. No sense in having a kid if you can't have yourself some fun with them." Nathan said that he wanted Julia dead before she found out some information about him. "What might that be? You holding out on her?"

"I have been, yes. I made a bit of money while I was married to her, and she's entitled to half of it. More if she tells anyone that those kids of mine are living with her." Duncan asked him what he'd won. "The jackpot, my friend. All the money in the world a man could spend. And it's going to be all mine as soon as she's gone."

Duncan wondered if the man knew that his kids would get her share of the money if Julia was dead but figured that he'd looked into things so didn't mention it. But he did think on getting some of the cash for himself — they were kind of related. The cops were too nosey right now, and he knew they were going to find something to bring him in again. This time they'd be extra careful about following the rules. And he'd be charged with murdering that kid they'd found too. That is, if they had any of Duncan's fluids, which he wouldn't part with while he'd been in the cell. Not one bit.

They talked about how they'd both been screwed by their wives. Duncan figured that he was the smarter of the two. Not only had he taken care of the wife, but he'd gotten away with it by the cops fucking up so badly when he'd been arrested. He told Nathan all about that.

"They said that it's because they didn't read me my rights. They did, but I guess they forgot to record it or something. When I told them that they'd not done that, lying through my teeth, they must have gone back and looked and couldn't find it. I was let out, but they're watching the shit out of me. My court lawyer said it was about mishandling the evidence of me being arrested. I have no idea, but I'm out and that's all that matters to me." Nathan told him that was a real shame. "Where is my sister, if you want her dead?"

"Believe it or not, she's right here in town with your other sister. Now there is a true bitch if there ever was one." Duncan thought all women could be bitches if you didn't knock them around enough. But he had firsthand knowledge of Hannah. She was terrible to him and for no reason at all. He told his new friend that. "Yeah, well, I tried that too. But it didn't do me any good. I had to get out of there, so I found me a new piece of ass and moved in with her. Now she's telling me that she's going to have my kid, and it's driving me nuts. At least I didn't marry this one."

"You do know that they're real close, right?" He nodded, reminding Duncan that they'd all been together at the wedding, and telling him that he'd tried to make each of them think the other was dead. "Yeah, didn't remember you until you showed me the picture, so don't go expecting me to perform miracles and recall someone else that might have been there. But that doesn't matter much now, does it? We have to figure out how to get you rid of my sisters and get me my son back here."

The more he thought about it, the more he wondered if he really wanted the kid back just for cleaning up after him. Christ, he'd had such a wonderful time killing that other boy. Duncan had thought it was his own at first, or he might not have had the simple pleasure of killing him. And when he'd figured it out, it was too late for the kid to be set free. If the police knew about that one, he was sure that he'd be back in the jail cell right now. Duncan thought them all fools. There wasn't any way that they could have missed that other body under there. Maybe if he got all rested up enough, he'd check to see if it was still there. That might be fun too, if it wasn't such hard work.

"There has to be a way to get to them. Your kid, is he stupid at all? I mean, can he be lured out with some candy or some shit?" He told him he doubted that Cody would trust anyone anymore. "Yeah, I've noticed that about my own kids. Even the baby—I haven't any idea what her name is at this point—she screamed every time I got near her. And I'd not touched her once yet."

Duncan told him that his kid was smart enough to stay hidden from him for about a month. And where he'd found him. Those Crosbys, they'd been a pain in his backside for a long time. They were forever bringing shit by his house for his wife and kid. What about him? he wondered. Why didn't someone think to bring him a case of beer, or even some fucking

59

jerky once in a while? For that matter, some cash. He'd surely like to have himself a bit of that right now.

Duncan had money too. Not millions, but he did have enough that he could buy and sell this land a couple of times and pay cash. Rose had found out about that too, the bitch, and had decided to have him pay for some extra food in the house, or maybe even get their kid a coat. It was winter, she'd told him with a tone.

But he'd not been able to get to the bank to get to the money, not right now anyhow. If the police saw him there, they'd start to wonder what he was doing and look into his life. His mom had left him that money and they had no business with it. He was glad now that he'd never taken it out of her name when she'd died. Just left it there and kept on using the card she'd given him. In the event of an emergency. She'd even had one made for Rose, for the new baby back then. But he'd nipped that in the bud too. No way was Rose going to get into his funds for shit. He'd not killed off his mom for nothing, by God.

Nathan left just before noon, saying that he had shit to do in town and was going to grab some lunch. He hadn't invited him to go along, which Duncan thought was sort of rude, but realized too that the man was half a cookie short of a whole one. Laughing at his own joke, he pulled out the bucket from under the sink and started filling it with water. He needed something clean to make his own meal on.

~~~

Elliot helped with the renovations as much as he could. The men that were there seemed to have a system going, and him being there was getting in their way. Backing away from what they were doing, he saw James coming his way. The little guy was working hard on making this venture of Elliot's a success.

"When they finish here, they'll be gone, true?" He said that they'd only fix the walls then go. "The others, they have worked on the lines for water. I must say, I had no idea what the water pressure was until today. The water comes out very fast, doesn't it?"

"Yes. Was anyone hurt?" He just waved him off, saying that it had been fun for them to ride the water spray. "You have warned them to be careful of the gas lines, haven't you? I don't want the place to go up in flames with you guys in here."

"Nay, we have left those alone for someone that knows about them." They sat there, James on his shoulder and Elliot on the gate of his truck. "Your mate, she was by yesterday, did you know that?"

"No, but then she can go wherever she wishes. You do know that she's the same as me, an immortal?" James said that they all did, but she could still get hurt. "Did something happen while she was here that I should be worried about?"

"Another man came by. He didn't speak to anyone here, not the men, but he did look as if he was searching for something. He smelled of the other man, Cody's sire." Elliot told him what his name was. "Nathan will be watched too. Why would he be here, searching as if he's lost something?"

"He's the ex-husband of Julia. We're not entirely sure what he's about, but we're keeping an eye on her and the children too. I know that he's been around for a couple of days, but that's about all I know. Emerald is looking into things for us, and you know that she'll be able to find anything if it's out there." James was afraid of her. He knew that she'd never harm him or the other faeries, but he was afraid of the control that she had over

61

the dragons. "If you see something out of the ordinary, you'll have to go to her if I'm not around. She's better equipped to take care of the man than any of us are."

"Yes, I know that. But the dragons, you see. We cannot go near them." He asked him why not, he thought that faeries and dragons got along. "We do, and some of us would love to be with them, but they're not something that any of us have cared for before. Do you think that her ladyship would allow us to talk to her about them?"

"I'm sure that she would. Or if she isn't someone you feel comfortable with—you know, with you being afraid of her—you can go to my brother Chase. He's the king." James looked at him then by flying in front of his face. Elliot was hard pressed not to laugh at the look on his face. "Well, you are afraid of her, aren't you?"

"I never said I was afraid. I'm afraid of the dragons and what they can do." He huffed, and Elliot had to look away. When he was upset like he was right now, James's wings would go so fast they were dizzying. "If you would be so kind as to tell her that I'd like to speak to her, I will show you how unafraid of her that I am."

"She's here now." James stood on his shoulder again, holding onto his earlobe very tightly. When he walked behind his head, hanging onto his hair so as not to be seen, Elliot was laughing when Emerald sat down beside him.

"I have some news for you and your mate." Elliot asked her what it was. "Did she ever mention money to you? Or her sister? Julia didn't act as if they had much, and from what I've been able to find out about her, she's been on the edge of poverty since before Nathan left them."

"But there is money." She said that there was a good deal of it. "How much? I mean, is there enough that it should have made a difference in the lives of those kids?"

"Their parents, Rose and Nathan's, died about two years ago, the mother's death under suspicious reasons. The will had been made out so they were to split the family fortune between the two of them, about five million dollars. Also, Rose was to get the house as well as any of the jewelry that was left. I'm not sure how he was the one that was in charge of the estate—it clearly states that Rose was to take care of it. But he was supposed to have sent his sister, Rose, the estate money that was to come to her because he'd been pressured by his attorney. I think she planned on using it to leave Duncan." He asked if she had cashed the check that came to her. "Yes, but here's the thing—I can't find it. It was cashed out, over a two-week period. The bank here in town wasn't able to give her all the cash at once. Her part in this was about three million after the sale of the cars."

"Okay, so he got about that much too. Why is he looking for Julia? I'm assuming that's what you wanted me to know." She said that was some of it. "Why is there always more when it comes to dealing with our mates' families, I wonder?"

"Because we can." He nodded and noticed that James had come to sit on his leg and was listening to them. "But there is more. During the marriage to Julia, he played the lottery. Every week without fail he would purchase fifty tickets with money that she made taking in sewing. We know that because he wouldn't touch the money in the account. I think it was because he wasn't going to tell her about the money for some reason. Anyway, he won, and she's entitled to half if not more of that money because she was his wife when he bought the tickets and won. And this is the real kicker in all this, Julia and Nathan aren't divorced. He never signed the last of the paperwork to get it finalized, so they were still married when this happened. It's a no-fault state—I didn't know what that meant for sure, but Jewel explained it to me. But he abandoned her and his children to pursue a romance with this other woman."

"If I remember correctly from when I was an attorney, she could also get him for child endangerment, simply because he had the means to make it so that they could have a better environment but didn't." Emerald smiled at him. "Whatever you're thinking, it can't bode well for anyone that is involved with this, does it?"

"Not everyone is on my shit list. But Nathan is. And here is something else you should be made aware of. Cody's father, he has money as well. Also left to him by his family. And since Rose is gone, we can't ask her if she knew about it. I'm assuming, and more than likely rightly so, that she didn't. Otherwise she might have been able to feed her son more and take better care of him." Elliot asked how much. "Millions. And while she was at home, barely making it and on government assistance, he was having himself a good old time without her. Also, since she'd applied for the assistance and received it illegally, and he was living with her at the time, he has to pay it all back. Including any and all money that should have gone for fees at the school, doctor bills, and anything else that they got help with while they were married."

"Holy shit." He tried to wrap his mind around how a person could do such a thing to his wife and son, but then realized that the two men were very similar and more than likely— He glanced at Emerald. "They're going to get together. Or they already have."

"They have. That's something else that I wanted you to know. But Hannah is just as much a target to them as Julia and the kids are. And Cody isn't safe either. I have looked in both their fucking sick heads. While I can't do shit about it right now, they are getting together on their need to be spouseless and childless." He asked her why she just couldn't take them out like she had the baby vamps. "There are rules that I have to follow too. They have to actually do something wrong for me to actually kill them, but they will, then I will."

James went to stand on her hand. His timing was off a little, but Elliot thought that if he fixed this with him, he'd be able to be less tense all the time. "James would like for you to allow him and his group to get to know the dragons."

"When?" James sputtered around and looked over at him, then back at Emerald. "You can talk to me. I'm not a monster unless you piss me off. And as far as I know, you've been avoiding me and my dragons."

"They frighten us all. We don't know much about their kind. But that isn't what I wish to talk to you about right now, my lady. This man, the one that is after young Cody, I have seen him and the other man here. And Cody's sire is the one that caused the fire. Had it not been for the faeries that were here then, I'm afraid that things would have been much worse." Emerald thanked him for helping. "It is our pleasure. But I have a desire to help you. All of us would like to. We have grown very fond of the young man and wish to keep him safe too."

"I'd like for you to assist in that as well, in keeping Cody from harm. And the other children too. There are five of them, counting Cody. Do you have people that would stay with them at all times, and be with them even after this is finished? It would be very important that these faeries had some magic, more than most. And we, the Crosbys, will need to be confident in your choice too. All right?" His little chest puffed out and Elliot watched as he went from terrified of Emerald to in awe of her. "When you have the time, sometime after we deal with these men, I'll show you the dragons and that they'd never harm anyone that is a part of this family. And as far as I'm concerned, you all are."

"Thank you, my lady. I was afraid that you'd turn us down. We're lowly faeries, as you know. But to us, we feel as if we were given a great honor when the Queen Kilian picked us to come here." She said that they were not lowly, and she'd hurt someone that said so. "You are very kind. Much nicer than I had first thought."

"Yeah, I can see where my exorbitant personality would cover that up."

They all laughed just as Hannah and Julia walked toward them. And the latter of the two had been crying a great deal, it seemed. Standing up, both he and Emerald went to the two women to find out what had happened.

I need you to come home when you got yourself a bit of time to sit and let me talk. He asked his dad why, what had happened. *You remember me telling you some time back about me buying a house? Well, we went to the bank today and we've bought six houses. They were on the auction block and we got too good of a deal not to have bought them. I'm hoping that we can put some of the people that come to us for help in them. But I'd like to give one of them to Julia and her children. I think they, of all people, need a place to call their own. And it costs us nothing to do this for her.*

Dad, that's a wonderful idea. He thanked him and said that it had been in his mind all along to help them, but he liked this way much better. *They're both here now, Julia and Hannah, but they look upset. I won't tell them what's going on, you should do that. But I'll talk to you later, all right?*

Yes, all right. I'm having the house cleaned as we speak. Also, Brandy and I are going to go do some shopping. I know that it's after Christmas and all, but I think they need something to celebrate. You take care of them and we'll do what we can here. He thanked his dad again but pulled Hannah into his arms. When she came easily, he believed things were much worse than he'd thought.

Chapter 5

"I'm going to hunt him down and break his fucking neck." Hannah watched her sister pace the big room in her house and wondered when she'd learned to curse like a sailor on leave. Looking over at Emerald and Jewel, she knew that they had something to do with it. When Julia spoke again, Hannah just let her. "He actually had money in the bank? All this time? What a dickweed."

"Fucktard is my favorite word." Hannah laughed when Emerald's husband, Chase, told her not to be encouraging. "I wasn't, I was simply telling her that I have a few words that she can use."

Emerald had told them what she'd been able to find out. Money, a great deal of it, had been there all along for Julia to use, and Nathan had kept it from her. Hannah wasn't sure if she shouldn't go out and break his neck herself. To be leaving those poor little kids without for so long.

"If I can get it fixed, you'll have a nice fat bank account in a couple of days. I have some friends at the bank who are going to take it out of his account and put it into yours, one that we'll set up for you today if possible." Julia asked Jason if that was legal. "You let us worry about the legalities on this. He should have been providing for you all along and he didn't. He's lucky that I don't snap his neck."

The boys, as Franklin called them, were seated around the living room, and she wondered, not for the first time, if they were this large because of the magic or did all vampires look like this. When Elliot said her name, she looked at him with a strained smile. There was too much going on, and he was much too calm about it. He asked her if she was all right.

"Actually, I'm very pissed."

Hannah asked him if he'd read her mind. "Yes. I needed to when you looked at me like you'd been hurt. So, you are aware of it, had Nathan hurt you when he saw you at the store, he wouldn't be breathing right now. I would have torn his throat out."

He was calm still, saying that about killing Nathan like it was no big deal. She was sure that it wasn't for him, that he might have had some experience in doing that sort of thing. But Hannah turned back to the family when thoughts of what he could do with his fangs on her flesh had her getting all warm again.

"There are any number of ways that he could have gotten into the place where you're staying. I should have thought about that when you asked to move out. I do hope that you'll reconsider staying with us until this is finished." Julia said that the kids had been so excited to have their own room in the small apartment that she couldn't do that to them just yet. Jason nodded, but told her that she'd have to be more careful. "He'll kill you if he gets the chance. We aren't for sure about this, but we believe that he murdered his mother too so that he could have the estate. And Rose would have gotten her share before she died — we just haven't been able to locate it as yet."

Franklin, who had only just shown up as the meeting was getting into full swing, stood up. He looked at her sister and smiled. Even from where she was sitting across the room from them, Hannah could see that he too was upset, but holding on to it better.

"This was going to be a surprise to you tomorrow, but we've — my family and I — purchased you a home." Julia started to protest. "I will be honest with you, my dear, even if I hadn't gotten a great deal on it, we would have helped you out like this. An apartment isn't safe. There are too many people there to let him in. Not to mention, when he does come back, and there is no reason to think that he won't, he might hurt someone else that lives there as well."

"But a house. I could barely afford food for my kids before this. Now, not only do I have the means and funds to take care of them, they'll have a yard to play in too. You've all been so kind to us. I don't know what to say."

Hannah went to her sister and held her while she cried. "Where is the house, Mr. Franklin? Is it close to us?" He told her that it was in the same neighborhood as her and Elliot, and that if she called him Mr. Franklin again, he was going to paddle her. "I'm trying. I promise."

He laughed with her as he described the home to them. "It's a big mammoth of a place. Six bedrooms and six baths. The kitchen is a dream come true, I was told. And there is a very large fenced in yard for them to play in. A swing set was left behind by the previous owners, and I'm having that checked out to make sure that it's steady for use."

"I will have to go shopping for beds and such." Chase, who had been quiet until then, cleared his throat and looked at Julia. "You didn't. Please tell me that you didn't furnish it as well."

"I'm afraid that we did. The place is furnished with beds and linens for them. Towels have been put away for each of the bathrooms. The things that were given to them have been put into the living room. We didn't want to pick out rooms for the kids, thinking that they'd get a kick out of that themselves. There is food being stocked in the pantry as we speak. Dad had the entire place cleaned by the faeries that work for Elliot, and it's spotless." Julia thanked them all. "We've fallen in love with your family and hope that you'll enjoy being here with us."

All Hannah could think about was that they'd done this for her sister for no other reason than that they could. She looked at Elliot, and when he turned to look at her, she could see something in his eyes that she'd never seen before on a man. He was in love with her. Just as he'd said several times today when they'd been out. She went to sit with him on the couch.

As Julia talked about getting a job and having money to feed them with, Hannah looked around the room that she'd only been in briefly last night. She'd been staying at the house that Elliot owned, while he was staying with one of his brothers. He didn't want to rush her, he'd told her. And true to his word, he hadn't. Not even to kiss her yet.

"You're thinking very hard. Should I have a look?" He was teasing her, another thing that he did well, always bringing a smile or laughter to her. She told him no, not this time. "Then perhaps you can share it with me. The expression on your face is hard for me to ascertain right now."

"I think I've fallen in love with you." Hannah felt her cheeks heat from embarrassment when he grinned. "I know you're thinking it's about time. But today, just now, I realized that you're nothing like any other person that I've known, not even humans."

"I've said this to you, but I wanted you to know that I do truly love you as well." She nodded, too emotional to think of anything but him. "We have a lot to learn about each other, and you need to be aware of what you have gotten in being my mate. But we have time, the rest of our long lives. And knowing that you *think* you love me, I can't tell you how happy you've made me."

When they glanced around the room again, Hannah really looked at it. There were enough antiques in there alone to have a collector's mouth water. The old and new blended well with each other. The rest of the house was the same. Modern, but not too much, with things that she'd bet were not only very old, but they more than likely were things that Elliot had chosen for himself.

The kitchen was the only room that she'd seen that didn't hold his touch. It was up to date and well cared for, but seldom used. Not because he didn't enjoy a fine meal, he told her, but because he'd been eating in town to save himself the cleanup.

Julia asked her if she'd come to her new home with her, to look around before the kids got back. They'd been staying with the pack, enjoying the outdoors with the young pups, she'd been told. A place that they'd been assured was the safest place for them. Even Hayley, who didn't say all that much, seemed

73

to be enjoying herself.

As they pulled on coats, since the weather had turned nasty again, she thought about things that she'd been doing for the last couple of days. It had been made much easier to do the things because she had money, according to Elliot, to get them done.

She had fielded phone calls from her boss. He'd been livid when she'd told him she wasn't returning for any amount of money and was writing her resignation and sending it on. Her tiny apartment was being closed up and her things were being brought to her. Even taking care of the arrangements for Rose had been easy with the support of the town.

Rose was related to her, not by blood but by marriage. And in turn, Cody was her nephew. But Elliot had talked to her about adopting him, giving him a good home and a better life than he'd had living with Duncan. She thought had he been living on the streets right now, it would've been better than living with his dad, but she told him she'd like that as well.

Cody was still shy about things. He always looked to her like he was waiting for someone to hit him, take away the things that he had. Or, and this one bothered her to no end, they were going to take away the food that he had on his plate and not feed him again. It broke her heart when she would hear him crying in his room at night. She could almost feel his pain about this.

The house for Julia was huge—old, but well-maintained. The kitchen wasn't as up-to-date as the one in Elliot's house, but her sister was thrilled to be able to cook good meals in it. She told her that she couldn't wait for the kids to see it. Hugging her sister, Hannah felt a little of her excitement wash over her as she made her way to Elliot.

He was talking to his brother about a business that they owned together. She had never seen a family, a strong opinionated family, get along as well as they did. When she was close enough to touch Elliot, he took her hand in his and kissed the back of it while continuing the conversation with Grayson.

"I think it would be worth it to see about enlarging the place and having it tooled out for a few more jobs." She didn't know what they were talking about but listened to them. Grayson smiled at her and brought her up to date on what was going on.

"So, you see, if they stay on the same track that they're on, they'll lose momentum when other companies try to duplicate what they're doing for a cheaper price. Also, and this is the kicker, them making them cheaper will ruin it for people like the Arnolds, who are making a good living on a good product."

"And how do you convince him? I don't think you'd be the type of people that would be hard hitting. What do you plan to help him see about the future?" Grayson looked at Elliot and she was embarrassed. "I'm sorry, this is none of my business."

"But it is your business. This is a family owned business that we run. You're a part of this family. Did you have something in mind? Before you answer that, you're right, he's not a hard-hitting sort of person. I've noticed that when backed into a corner, he has no opinion about whatever it is that we were talking about, and he will walk away with his head down in shame. He might well be a smart man, just inherited a mess. Or he could be someone that has been run over most of his life and doesn't know how to stand up for himself and the people that work for him." She asked him what the business was. "They make frames. Not the kind that you pick up in a store, but custom ones. Here, let me show you."

There was a frame on the mantle in the living room. Grayson handed it to her and it took her only a moment to feel the quality of the thing. And it was simply beautiful. Touching the wood that looked like it had been made from several different kinds of wood pressed together, Hannah asked what they'd do with this if they were to retool the company.

"Bowls. I've seen them there. They make them for the employees each year for Christmas." He left again and came back with a box that he set on the floor. After handing her one of the medium sized bowls, Grayson continued. "They're not in a production place to make these in any quantity. The company works on these, a few a month until they get enough to give away. Each year there is a different bowl that is like that frame."

The workmanship was exquisite. The curve of the bowl was similar to that of a man's body. She loved the feel of it when she ran her fingers over it, and then Hannah dipped her hand into the inside and felt the smoothness of the wood and was sure it was the love of the person who made it.

"The man that owns the company, he's the one that makes the bowls, isn't he?" Grayson said that he was. "I thought so. Only a person that loved someone very much could have made this. I'd say that's why he doesn't want to retool or expand in this line. He makes them—they're his babies, so to speak, and a part of him that he gives to the people that take the time to work with him. If I were you, I'd do something different than the bowls to retool it. I'd say cutting boards. Also, I saw in a company once where a man had a set of paper blocks on this desk, so that he could build things and knock them over. A stress reliever, if you ask me."

"Cutting boards would be made to look like the wood on this frame?" She told Elliot that was what she'd do. "Each piece would be unique in not just the curves of the wood, but also the way that it came together when they pressed them."

"What did you do before this? I'm sure that I should know that, but I can't remember if we were told." Grayson would have known what she did. She was sure that she'd been investigated — there wasn't any way that a family with this much money would let someone take them. Hannah told him that she had a degree as an engineer, but her talent was wasted for a company that made high end gifts for people. "Engineer? So, you did what? Went to companies and showed them what you wanted?"

"No, I went to them to see what sort of deal we could make with them. In my job as a researcher, I had all the answers to questions that they might have. From how production would be affected if they didn't do whatever it was they wanted, all the way to how much they could expect as an increase in profits. But our company was to have exclusive rights to some new-fangled toy that the rich and stupid have to have to show off. It made them both a great deal of money." Elliot asked her why they didn't let her try and make things that would work. "You'd think that, wouldn't you? But no, my boss — Parker Shaw is his name — said that I was too pretty and sexy to have in an office all day. I made good money, very good money, but I rarely got to spend any time at home to enjoy the benefits of having some. Not a great deal, not like you guys, but enough that I could afford popcorn with my movie should I have the time to go. Why?"

"You need to work for us." She told Ryan when he joined

them that she didn't know what she could do for them. "For one thing, you could help with this business. Design the blocks that Grayson was telling me about. Then help with getting them polished enough that we don't have to close up this company we're working with. It'll keep a lot of people working."

Sean and Jason joined them then, and she had the most overwhelming need to run. But Elliot took her hand into his and she calmed down, felt herself breathe easier. And with that, she was also able to listen without panic.

"Right now, this business is on the verge of closing up. The frames that they make are unique, beautiful, and priced well. But they're still only frames. There are dollar stores across the country that could make them cheaper and sell them at a cheaper in price." She asked if they had a sales rep for this sort of thing. "No. To be honest, I don't think any of us thought of that before. Instead of retooling some business, perhaps they just needed a fresh bunch of customers to add to their baseline. No, that has never occurred to me before. See, you've helped us already."

"That wasn't help, that was common sense. Stop looking outside the box so far that you lose sight of the fucking point." She looked at Emerald when she laughed. "Does she always find it funny when someone takes you to task?"

"Pretty much. And I love her for it." Jason looked all mushy when he glanced at Jewel. They were a beautiful couple, as were Chase and Emerald. Hannah was afraid to look at Elliot, afraid of what she might see there if she did.

After they kept trying to convince her that she really did need to work for them, Hannah went to find her sister. She was in the kitchen, just sitting at the bar that was in there. She said her name softly and was glad to see her smiling as she turned.

"The kids will love being here, don't you think?" She said that she thought they would. "Nathan had money. All the time we were together. When the kids needed something for school he'd tell me that there wasn't any way that he was paying for shit when he already paid taxes. That never made sense to me as he hadn't worked for as long as I knew him, so he never paid any. You have no idea how hard I had to work, just to make it so they had a minimal amount of food in their bellies each day."

"He's going to be really pissed off when he figures out that you got the money, isn't he?" Julia nodded. "I promise you, Julia, he's never going to hurt you any more. Even if I have to go to prison for killing him."

"Don't do that, please. I just found you again. I couldn't stand it if you were taken from me because of Nathan." Hannah went to the cabinets and pulled down two cups and a tin of loose leaf tea. "You remembered that I like tea when I'm stressed."

When she'd been to the other homes, she had noticed that they all kept the same brand of tea in the same spot in the kitchen. Even the little teacups were in the same place. Hannah figured since Franklin had been part of the shopping spree. he'd have bought Julia the same thing. And then, without thinking, put it where he'd always had at his own home. She looked at her sister as she waited for the water to get hot.

"I do. And it's a small wonder that you have left any tea for the rest of the world as stressed out as you seem to be." She laughed, as Hannah had hoped that she would. After making the tea and giving her the lovely cup and taking her own, she sat down beside her at the bar. "I'm in love with Elliot. I wasn't sure at first, but he's a good man. All of them are."

"I know that you're in love with him, and I do believe they are the nicest people I've ever known. But Hannah, this isn't their fight. He's coming after me, not them." She sipped her tea while trying to think of a way to tell her what her opinion was. "The kids are already calling them uncle. And for the first time in months, Hayley is sleeping all night. I owe that to them. I just don't want to see them hurt."

"Okay, I'm going to tell you like I see it, all right?" Julia laughed and told her to go for it. "Good. You're a fucking idiot. More than him, I think. You've got this amazing family that not only makes sure that you're all heathy and well cared for, but they bought you a fucking house. A big fucking house. And on top of that, they've found you sitters so you can finish your education and gave you a car to get back and forth with. When they tell you that you're going to be safe, I'd believe them. And so, what the fuck if they aren't your real family? If you remember correctly, we didn't have it half as good as they've given your kids. So when they say to you, Julia, we've got your ass in this, you say thank you, I couldn't do it without you. You do not tell them this isn't their fight. I think they'd kill for you."

"We would." They both turned to see Elliot standing in the doorway to the kitchen. "My family has left. Jason is going to pick up the kids from school at the pack so that he can bring them back here. My dad said that they'd be back at dinnertime for pizza and donuts. His favorite human food since we were changed."

Elliot came into the room with them, gliding across the floor like the man that he was. Wealthy. Confident. And ready, more than ready, to take on the world if necessary. When he kissed her on the mouth, a quick taste of him lingered on her

80

lips long after he moved to make himself a cup of tea. Hannah was so messed up in her mind that she almost missed what he was saying.

"What did you say?" Elliot turned to look at her as the water was put to boil. "Did you just say that Duncan and Nathan are in on something?"

"Yes." Elliot kissed her again, this time on the nose before continuing. "Nathan went to see Duncan earlier this morning. They talked for a little while, and when he left a few hours later, Duncan seemed to search for something in the house. It wasn't until later that we figured out it was the food card that Rose used. Unless Nathan told him about the money — then he'd be looking for that too. But for some reason, I don't think it's in the house. Not that one anyway."

"It's not loaded." Julia flushed. "What I mean is, I called and canceled it a few days ago. And then Emerald called them back to get them to hustle their asses up before it was used. She can move mountains, can't she? I didn't figure that with Rose gone and Cody living here, there was any point in leaving it for someone to steal and lose. I hope that was all right."

"I'm betting that if she set her mind to it, she could at that. And yes, that was perfectly fine. I'm glad that you thought of it." Elliot sat with them; his hands looked so much larger holding the delicate teacup in his hand. "Now, I've spoken to James — he's the faerie that works with me in the greenhouse. He is going to bring by some faeries from his pip to have you see which ones might be good fits for your children. And for you as well. Cody is getting to know his companion now."

"Pip?" Elliot explained to her that it was what a group of faeries were called. "And these would be tiny people, correct?

81

How do you think they can help them if trouble comes? I'm not saying that they couldn't help, I just don't know how they'd stand up to two grown men who don't have the good sense to quit while they're ahead."

The shrill whistle made her jump a little. The little person that landed on the table in front of them bowed before them all and turned to look at Julia. Hannah didn't know why, but she thought that he was sizing her up for something. Perhaps, as Elliot had said, so they could have a faerie around them all the time.

"You've had a very hard life, my lady. I'm sorry for that. I think that you'd do well with some sunshine in your life, what do you say?" Her sister nodded and put out her hand to touch the little guy. "You can pick me up. Lord Elliot carries me around on his ear most of the time."

Laughing, Julia picked him up and held him face to face with her. "You're very right, sir. I've had a hard time of it. But it's been pointed out to me that I should be leaning more on the help I have instead of whining about how much they might get hurt."

"Yes, you should. But you should know a few things about yourself. You are like the rest of them." Julia frowned. "Immortal, my dear. As part of this family, the lady Kilian thought that it would be a shame for you to leave our hearts one day. And your children are the same. You also have a wee bit of magic to call upon should you need it. Lady Emerald, she gave that to you when she touched you."

"What sort of magic?" James told her to touch the side of her cup, gently like. And when she did, it filled to the brim with hot tea again. "I can make myself a cup of tea whenever I want?"

"He's trying his best to go slowly with you. He's not used to humans all that well." Elliot told James to tell her what she had. "You will have this and more as you get older too, just like we do as vampires."

James told her sister to think of the pot of flowers on the sink. When she did, he got off her hand and told her to bring it to her. The pot rumbled around a little before it came to her and landed in her hand.

"That's fantastic." He told her that she didn't have to see whatever she wanted, just call for it and it would be there. "My car keys and cell phone too? I'm forever losing them."

James told her that she'd be able to do that easily. "And the faerie that I have in mind for you, she'll be a good match. Her name is May. She'll introduce the children to their faeries too. They've been around them a good deal since coming here, so don't expect them to be afraid."

"I won't. And I'm not anymore." James nodded, and her sister looked at her. "You're right. I need to depend on the rest of your family to help me. And learn again how to make decisions on my own. Thank you, Hannah. You're a pain in my ass, outspoken to a fault, but I love you dearly."

Hannah told her that she loved her as well and decided that she needed to tell someone else that. She only hoped that he didn't make fun of her when she did. But she didn't think that Elliot would. He was a good man, and she suddenly thought that she couldn't do any better if she had a lifetime of looking.

Chapter 6

Elliot was going to have to talk to Hannah soon about his needs. He wasn't desperate yet, and he didn't want to get that way. She went into the house ahead of him, then turned when she was in the hallway. He felt his body tense up, wondering what she'd seen. When she wrapped herself around him, Elliot pressed her to the wall and took over the kiss that she had started.

It occurred to him, only for a moment, that the front door was still open. They were in the great entrance hall where anyone could see them. But instead of letting any of that worry him, he took what she was offering, and to hell with everything else.

Her body was hot. Her hands were tangled in his hair and clothing. When her breast was finally bared to him, he lifted her higher and suckled it into his mouth. The need to bite her there had his fangs stretching in his mouth. He lifted his head from her and looked at her.

"I want to taste you. Everywhere." The nod wasn't what he wanted, Elliot needed to hear the words from her. "Tell me, Hannah. Tell me that I can bite you and make you mine."

"Please, Elliot. I'm on fire for you. Bite me, drain me, just fill me so that I can feel like a woman." Her voice had turned harsh, raspy for her begging him. But he wanted all of her, not just a fuck in the hallway.

He leaned back down and toyed with her nipple. When it hardened more just for him, he took the small morsel into his mouth and sucked harder. Her scream of release was just what he'd been waiting for, and he sank his fangs into her full breast.

She tasted of honey and warm sunshine. Her blood not only filled his mouth, but as he swallowed it down, he could almost feel it filling his body. His cock, hard before, now seemed to strain at his body. He needed to come, in her or on her, but he needed his release too.

Moving quickly through the house, he had her in their bedroom in seconds. Stripping off the remaining bit of her clothing made his beast roar at him to hurry, to mark her as theirs. Taking her to the bed, he thought of slowing, giving her as much pleasure as he could before he took his own, but she wrapped his cock in her hand and held him tightly.

"I'm going to taste you. Lick your lovely cock until you hurt with it." He told her that he did already. "Then this should be easy for you. Come down my throat, Elliot. I've thought of nothing else today but having you fuck the life out of me and swallowing you down my throat."

The moment that she took him into her mouth, he was lost. Begging her to let him take her fell on deaf ears. And when she fisted him, he held his breath when she let him slide to the back of her throat, then swallowed.

Elliot knew that he'd been close to coming anyway. His balls were tight against his body — they ached, they were so full. But the moment that she tightened around his cock, Elliot had never experienced so much pain and pleasure at the same time. And then he came.

It was like he'd had his head removed for the power of his climax. He held on tightly to the end of the bed, his nails tearing into the hard wood enough to mark it. Elliot felt his knees weaken then. His heart was beating hard enough that he was sure that his family could hear it in their homes. Hannah lifted her head and looked at him, and Elliot fell in love with her all over.

"My turn."

He helped her onto the bed better, touching her everywhere he could, not just tasting her skin, but tasting her deeper. Tiny bites of her made her moan, and in turn did the same to him. He was going to make this last, he told himself. It was what he'd wanted since he met her.

Elliot lifted her arms and put them above her head. With him suckling at her breast, her hips rotated toward him. Running his hands down her arms, licking the strong muscle there, Elliot could taste the difference of her skin where it was tender.

He moved up her body with his own. Holding himself at the entrance of her heat, he said her name until she looked at him. Her eyes were dazed looking, her body covered in a fine sheen of sweat, as his was. He could hear her heart beating as fast and as hard as his own.

"One day I'd like to change you into what I am." She

nodded quickly, like she'd been thinking of that as well. "We'll take our time with it, changing you a little each time we make love."

"Elliot, I want to be able to bite you, taste you as I've never done before." Her voice was sexy, a little harsh as well. When she begged him once more, all he could think about was making her his, forever, like he was. But he'd seen it happen before — too fast and she would die. Too slowly and she would die as well.

He licked around her throat, tasting her pounding pulse from her skin, and bit down. He'd tasted her before, in the hallway earlier. But this was different. Even his beast could tell that her blood was richer, thicker in her veins. Even her smell had changed since downstairs.

Sucking hard on the tiny wounds that he put there, he entered her, sliding forward until his balls touched her. He wanted to roar out that she was his, to let the world know that he'd taken his mate. As he drank greedily from her, he knew that he could never let her go. She was his forever, so long as they both lived.

Sealing the wounds where he'd drank from her, Elliot made love to her. Softly he said her name, telling her how much he loved her. He told her how her skin tasted, how much he loved the way her nipples responded in his mouth. All the while, he slid in and out of her, filling them both with some kind of carnal need that only they could fulfill for each other.

Her nails dug into his back when she came again and again. When she begged him for a taste of him, he sliced open his throat and let her take as much as she could. And when she licked over the wound that he'd made for her, his cock stretched more. He felt like he'd been shot out of a cannon for the way it had made him feel.

"Take me."

He could no more not do that than he could harm her. Lifting her ass up to meet his downward strokes, he fucked her hard, his stronger body pounding her until she screamed twice more that she was coming. And when she said that she loved him, shouting out that she was his, Elliot came a second time and felt his world tilt off its rhythm.

Dropping atop her, he held her to him as his body convulsed and shook with the release. Her own tightened around him too, to the point that he wanted to beg her to please stop. Rolling to his side, he took her with him, pulling the blanket over them both, and fell into a deep sleep.

When he woke the room was pitch black. Not even the moon, which had been up when they'd made their way home earlier, was shining its beam into their room. Elliot reached for Hannah, and finding her safe and sound and lying beside him, he closed his eyes again and thought he could stay there for the rest of his life with his very lovely mate next to him.

The next time that he woke, the room was bright with sunlight. Someone had opened the curtains to his room, and he had to blink several times to see that he was alone in the bed as well as the room. Getting up, his body slightly sore from what they had done last night, he reached out for Hannah and found that she was upset.

Are you all right? She didn't answer him, and he'd forgotten that he'd not told her that they could do this. *I'm sorry, love. You only need to think of one of us and you can speak to them without any trouble. With me, we can share some memories too, but not with the others.*

I have to tell you that I think I've made the biggest mistake in my life saying that I'd help your brothers. They're bombarding me with question after question, and I want to fucking bash in a couple of heads. I'm with Jason and Sean right now, and I guess the rest are coming in too. He laughed, and felt her humor retuning as he stepped under the spray of the shower. *I wasn't sure if I should wake you or not. You seemed to be sleeping so soundly.*

I was. But I was really disappointed in not waking with you beside me. What time did you get up? Elliot knew that it was just after seven in the morning. And while he was usually up much earlier, he wondered if she was a morning person too. *Did you have breakfast?*

Yes, they bought me breakfast when they found me downtown at five thirty. I have no idea why I was awake at that time, but I decided that I've been lax enough and went for a run. I didn't get all that far before I met up with them. By the way, this town is in serious need of some kind of Danish place. Or bagels. I asked for one from the restaurant in town, and I think she thought I was talking gibberish. He laughed. *I was wondering if you were coming into town later. I need to hit a few of the local stores here for some shampoo and such. While I love the way yours smells, it's not very nice on me. Your brothers pointed out that I smell like you.*

Elliot laughed before explaining. *They know that we had sex, that we're a mated couple. That's what they meant by smelling me. You'll be able to smell them too, I think, at least that's what Jewel told me once when she had a question about how the scents were now stronger.* She asked him if they'd know every time the two of them had sex. *No, and they don't actually know that we had sex really, just that the two of us exchanged blood and became one.*

If you think about it, that's sort of creepy. Oh, before I forget, you and I have to go to the courthouse sometime today to sign some paperwork to have us investigated. I think it's about Cody, but I don't know. He asked her who she'd spoken to. He had no idea who it might have been, because his had already been taken care of before Hannah had come here. And then soon after, he'd contacted the adoption agency and had Hannah investigated as well. *I don't know. I was leaving the house when the phone rang. I was excited about getting out in the snow so I didn't really pay attention to much of what he was saying. I wrote some things on the chalkboard by the phone, but it's been a hell of a morning so far.*

I want you to tell my brothers what you just told me. She asked him if something was wrong. *I'm not sure at this point, but I don't want to take any chances with you. Tell them that I'll see what you've written down before I come there.*

He looked at the board when he got to the kitchen. He had no idea why he'd left it there when he remodeled the kitchen, but was glad for it now. As he read over her notes, he finally took a picture of it with his cell phone and sent it to Jason. He was working downtown most of the time, and he might have a clue who this Mr. P was. Something was going on, and he'd bet his last month's income that it had to do with Duncan and Nathan.

Driving calmly toward the offices where he knew his family was, he tried to think if there was any reason for the agency to contact them. But as he was pulling into the lot, something else occurred to him—it had been before seven when she'd been called. No one in those offices were there until nine or after. As soon as the place opened up, he was going to make a call to find out what was going on.

~~~

Nathan had to make sure that his ex-wife didn't find out about the money he had. Not just the lottery money, but also the estate. He wished now that he'd not told the other moron, Duncan. The guy seemed to have a one-track mind when it came to dealing with their families. He only had one brat to get rid of—Nathan had a wife and four brats to murder off. This shit was getting on his nerves.

He had gotten the phone number of the household from some woman downtown. The florist shop wasn't going to be opening any time soon, he thought with a laugh. Knocking her around a bit had been a little disappointing, but he did get what he wanted. He hadn't tried to figure out her name—it wasn't what he'd wanted from her. But he did get into her private files, as she called them, and had found a lot of phone numbers he'd bet no one else had.

It was a stroke of genius to have called Julia's sister. He knew that if anyone could make Julia come to heel, it would be Hannah. Not that Nathan thought she'd be easy; every time he'd tangled with her before, she'd come out on top. She not only hit like a man, she fought like one too. Dirty and mean.

He waited in the shadows for Hannah to come to him. He'd told her there was paperwork to sign off on and that she had to be there at eight. Government offices, he knew for a fact, didn't have anybody in them until nine, or even after.

Nathan hadn't any idea that she was adopting Duncan's kid, and wondered if the man knew it himself. That would be fun to tell him, Nathan thought. Just to see the look on his face when he did it. More for him to hold over his head.

The woman and the man walking on the sidewalk didn't

bother him. They were those yuppie types that wore workout clothing yet never broke a sweat. Dismissing them, he pulled out the letter he'd gotten from the post office yesterday. This shit was going to be taken care of as soon as he was done with Hannah.

Somehow, his wife had found out about his money. And not only that, but the letter he'd gotten from the attorney representing her had said that she was going to get half, if not more, of his winnings. He'd not even gone public with that shit yet, and here she was with all the information that he had.

Like she knew the exact date the he'd purchased the winning ticket, at what store, as well as how many other tickets he'd bought. Most of them had been scratch offs, but he'd won a bit with some of them too. It even mentioned that — the instant winnings that he'd had that day. He didn't like her being up in his business. What he did with his money was his affair.

He looked down the street again when he heard someone talking.

"Hello, numb-nuts. How's it hanging?" He almost didn't recognize the woman speaking, but once she introduced him to the man next to her, he knew that Hannah had called someone else after he'd talked to her. "You've nothing to say? Well, I have plenty. But I won't. I'm going to let you try and figure out how much more I know about you and your little scheme to get to Julia and her kids."

"They're not her kids, but mine. And I want her to come home so that I can teach her what it's like to fuck with me."

The punch to his face had him staggering back. He might have been able to blame his misfortune on the man, but he was still leaning against the wall where he had been.

"You letting a woman fight for you, fuck wad? Figures. Men like you and your kind were always pussies."

When the man yawned, just really opening his mouth, Nathan took a second step back. The fucking bitch had brought a vampire. What the fuck would she go and do something like that for? Nathan looked at Hannah and wondered just how far he could push her before the vamp stepped in. He decided that he wasn't going to take the chance. Today anyway.

"You're to stay away from Julia and her kids. And since you left them with her when you decided to find something greener, she has taken custody of them in the eyes of the law. By the way, you should be more careful about signing off on paperwork when it's sent to you, moron." Nathan asked her what she was talking about. "I'm not your sitter. Figure it out for yourself. And I'm glad to see that you've heard from her attorney. That'll make things go so much smoother for her when you go to court."

"I'm not going to court, and you tell her I said to drop this shit right now, or so help me, she won't be able to hide from me." Hannah laughed and pointed out that she already had. "I'll find her. You want to know why? Because you're going to tell me where she is. I know for a fact that you're the heavy here, he can't go where I can. And I'll take you out in the sunlight and fuck with that pretty face of yours."

"You think I'm pretty? Not that I care, but that's the first time you've ever said anything nice to me." She turned to Crosby and smiled at him. Nathan wondered in that brief moment if a woman had ever looked at him that way. "You see, Nathan here hates me. No reason why, other than I tried to protect my sister from him right after they got married. She called me, I came to her. It was the last time I heard from her until idiot here told me she was dead."

"That's not nice." Nathan nearly rolled his eyes at the man, but decided that the look he was giving him now said that he'd better rethink a great many things. Not just rolling his eyes. "Did you know that once a vampire gets old — and I am, very much so — they can do all sorts of things that humans might not know? For instance, I can stand the sunlight better than any other vampire I know, with the exception of my family. You might want to consider that when you threaten my wife about harming her."

"Wife? You married this fucking bitch? Holy Christ man, what were you think — ?"

His throat was suddenly closed off. The tightening of something around him was squeezing the life out of him. And trying to peel at it, move whatever was making him not able to breathe, just wasn't working.

"You really are all kinds of stupid, aren't you?" The man's voice was calm, soft even. But it didn't sound any less threatening than if he had shouted at him. "I'm going to let you go, and you're going to tell Hannah how very sorry you are that you called her a bitch. Also, you will remember what this feels like if you go near Julia or those kids again. Blink if you understand."

Nathan blinked several times and could see pinpoints of black spots before his eyes. When he was suddenly free, he fell to the ground, holding his throat and wondering when the hell he'd lost control in this situation. He had to think, to regroup. Standing up, he nearly walked away when Crosby cleared his throat. Nathan turned and looked at Hannah, and wanted to smack the shit out of her more than he ever had his wife.

"I'm sorry that you forced me to call you a bitch." He looked over at the man again when he told him to behave. "All right, I'm sorry that you were ever born so that I had to call you a bitch."

"You're not going to live very long if you keep pissing me off." Again, his voice was calm, like he had just told him that the weather was nice and that they expected sunshine to fly out of his ass. "Tell her."

He couldn't have stopped himself from dropping to the ground if he had wanted to, Nathan thought. There wasn't any way that he could have fought off the desire to want—no need—to tell her that he was sorry, either. Looking up at Hannah, he had the most insane desire to go against the large vampire and smack her where she stood. Instead, he told her that he was sorry, that was all, and left it at that.

When he found himself alone, Nathan stood up. He had no idea when they had gone; for all he knew, he could have been sitting in the melting snow for hours. Stretching his neck, he felt the pull at his throat and ran his fingers over the pain. When his fingers came away bloodied, he stared at it on his fingers.

He'd been bitten. By a vampire. Walking away from the courthouse where he'd been waiting, his mind went over every detail that he'd heard about being bitten by one. He knew one thing for sure—the vampire would know his every thought, his every move from now on. At least until he was able to kill him.

I'm afraid that won't work for me. Nathan stood very still when the voice in his head spoke. *You are fucking with the wrong family, Nathan. So whatever you have in your head right now, you should consider rethinking it. For your own sake.*

"She's mine to do with as I please. There isn't a court in the world that won't agree with me." The laughter made his balls tighten to his body, his blood seemed to stop flowing. "You don't scare me none. I've killed your kind before."

No you haven't. Don't lie to me when I have a front row seat to all your misdeeds and lies. You've only ever killed one thing in your life, and that was when you ran over a squirrel — and then you cried like a small child when you saw it. Since then, you've hired others to do your misdeeds. Nathan thought about running, getting away from this with his body intact. But Crosby spoke again. *You cannot hide from me, Nathan Henry. I will be able to find you even if you were to be torn apart by the pack that roams the property where your lovely wife lives.*

He believed him too. As he made his way back to where he'd parked his car, he thought of all the things that he'd have to do now. The money and getting it hidden was going to be the first thing he took care of. There wasn't any way that Julia or those kids were going to get a penny of it. Not so long as he had breath in his body.

Which won't be that long, so you know, if you continue thinking like that. I foresee me having to bring you to your early death, don't you? You're not the type of man that anyone would miss either, just so we're clear on that. He asked him about his kids and wife. *No, not them even. I think, and this could just be me, that they're quite happy where they are. The children have their own rooms, a yard to play in, and food in their bellies whenever they want it. And that little Hayley? Well, it does my heart a world of good when she calls me Uncle Elliot. They all are very dear to me. I'm telling you right now, Nathan, you hurt those children or Julia again, the police will look at the mess that I make of your body and have nightmares about it.*

He believed him. He had no idea why, but he believed that the vampire would be true to his words, and not only kill him with a vengeance, but make him suffer as well. Nathan decided to go to his parents' home, the one that he went to when he wished to have fun without Julia knowing about it. Christ, this was a cluster fuck if there ever was one.

Once he was at his family home, he began to feel better about things. And since he'd been able to distance himself from the vampire, he began to believe, or at least tell himself, that he wasn't as big a threat as he'd made himself out to be. The vampire wasn't going to be a problem, he thought to himself, and went into the living room.

Nathan wet his pants when he saw him there. Just standing in his living room like he belonged. Mother fuck, he was going to die, he just knew it.

"You'll learn that I'm not one to fuck with." Crosby spoke so quietly Nathan wasn't sure that it was him who'd spoken, but when he came at him, Nathan simply blacked out.

Chapter 7

The building was in good shape. The machinery was as well. When she asked to see how small of a slice the cutter could make, Mr. Peel was glad to help. She wondered briefly how easy it would be to get her brothers-in-laws here to slice them up.

Not really. She had grown to love their overbearing and old-fashioned ways of doing things—even the way that they treated her, like she was soft glass. But by the same token, she hated their overbearing ways and their old fashion ways of doing things—and especially hated that they treated her like she was going to break at the slightest thing.

"This thing that you think we can do, do you believe that it will save the company?" Mr. Peel wasn't a young man—she guessed that he was in his mid-fifties if not a little older. And when she'd first came in today, he'd been anything but polite. But after talking to him for an hour, showing him what she had in mind, he had changed his tune and was now showing her around the large impressive building.

"I think it's a start in the right direction. And with this work, you'll be able to continue repaying the money that the Crosbys lent you, as well as meet your other deadlines." She looked at the slice of beautiful wood when he gave her the thin strip. "It will need to be about an inch square when it's a finished product."

"We can go smaller if you want, but the detail on the way we put together wood would be lost. One inch will still show the coloring of the different woods but be small enough for what you have in mind." She nodded and watched as he picked up several of the other slices that he'd had made for her and followed him to another department.

That was something that she needed to talk to him about as well—they needed to have their departments closer or have a runner. A runner to take the product to the next department rather than the man who just worked on the piece carry it to the next step in the process. She asked him about that as they moved across the manufacturing building.

"If, say, you have one person to run multiple pieces to the next step, they can all be working more instead of waiting on the next piece. You will still be able to make them by hand, and with the quality of work that the country has come to expect from you, but it would be easier work and faster." He nodded, and she knew that he was considering it rather than saying or doing what she wanted. Mr. Peel was an introvert, someone that she could relate to on his level. "And you could put a few more people on your payroll to show that you're expanding. And that, more than anything, is what investors want to see."

"We'd have to do interviews too, I'm guessing." She knew

that was the reason for him being so short-staffed. "I don't know a lot about interviewing anymore. When my dad started this place, he just let anyone that needed work come in. Now, well, I'm a little on the shy side, in case you didn't notice, and I've not been very good at it."

"We have a firm that we can work with on getting you people that you can not only trust, but will also do a good job. You, for now, only need someone that is able to lift and tote for you. Someone that can, perhaps, load things onto a small vehicle and take the product to the next step." He nodded and said that he thought that might work better for him. "Good. And Mr. Peel, I'd suggest you find yourself a replacement for Mrs. Parker. She's antiquated in her way of doing things, and the fact that she refuses to use a computer to put in orders is hurting your bottom line."

"I know that, but she worked for my dad. And he thought the world of her." Hannah said that she was a very sweet woman, but she was also set in her ways and needed to be replaced. "I'll need someone to replace her too, I guess. I know that you're only trying to help, but some of these people have been here since the beginning, when my dad owned it."

"Mr. Peel, there is a man right now stretched out on one of your lines fast asleep. Every day he comes in and goes straight to the line that you no longer use and takes his rest time. At lunch, when the bell goes off to take their time off, he wakes, goes to eat, then comes back to do the same until quitting time. Those sorts of people have been doing this since your father was here. And this man, he has it in his head that you're going to follow in the same steps. He's eating away at your profit line. Shall I go on, or do you want me to just give you a list? I've been here for less than a day, and I've seen seven people of the two hundred that you employ taking advantage of you."

He stopped walking and leaned against the wall that made up an office that some used to have a quickie with one of their fellow employees—also a place where naps were taken. He glanced around the floor, seeing things, she'd bet, with fresh eyes. Mr. Peel looked at her, and seemed to have gotten some inner strength in that moment.

"You said you'd hire me other people, ones that will be willing to work for a day's pay?" She said that the firm would do that gladly. That was one of the things that she'd talked over with Chase and Jason yesterday. "From where I've been standing, Mrs. Crosby, you might well have to hire me a whole new crew to come in and be trained. That'll put me behind in making the big payment. I can see this working and I'm willing to put myself out there, but it'll do me no good whatsoever if I do this all for nothing."

"I'll talk to them right now. All right?" He nodded and straightened, the pieces of wood in his hand forgotten. "You go finish that up for me, so I can show my partners, and I'll work on this."

Reaching out to Chase and the rest of the family, she told them what she'd told Mr. Peel. She wondered, not for the first time, how they'd gotten around her and got her to be the front man for them. Making her a full partner had helped, and the job that they were going to help Julia get as well. Hannah wondered if she had sucker written across her forehead.

Nah, I would have told you if you do. I'm nice like that. She wanted to find Chase and show him what a nice person she wasn't. *You're very mean when you want to be, aren't you? I think that's why we love you so much. Honey, just give us a minute while we discuss this. You can speak to them as well.*

They talked for the next ten minutes. She interjected only when it was necessary. Emerald told her of the others that were resting up on the job, and she made a note on the small computer she was using. It made things easier for her than a notepad and pen.

Franklin had the voice of reason and calmness. She'd heard that he'd not always been like that. Complaining about not being able to join his mate had made him a sour man. But he'd changed, almost overnight, Elliot had told her.

Jason was the thinker. He'd only say what he had in mind after he'd worked over every angle and did the math in his head. And when he spoke, the others tended to listen to him. She thought that of all of them, he had the best ideas about working with the businesses.

Chase was always joking. But when he needed to be firm he could in a second too. Like Franklin, he'd not always been that way. Emerald had brought out parts of them that he told her had been long buried. With his wife, he had also gained a new outlook on life.

Hannah was in awe of Grayson. He could make a computer do whatever he wanted. Writing programs for them had come as naturally to him as breathing. Games too. That was what he did in his spare time, write programs for game systems that made him millions each year.

Ryan was quiet, but not when he had to work out a project. She could see him now, pacing the room and tossing out ideas, only to have them nixed by himself. He had kept up with his law degree and used it for his family. He could also type like he'd been trained by the best. She loved to watch him work best of all.

Sean was harder to read than the rest of them. She knew that he was a people watcher, that he enjoyed sitting for hours in the mall to see how people reacted to different situations. Hannah also knew that he had the tenderest heart. He cared for wounded animals, nursing them back to health until they could be returned to the wild. For some reason, Hayley had attached herself to the man, and he seemed to enjoy it a great deal.

Hannah thought of her mate, Elliot. He could and would be the heavy in most situations. It appeared to everyone else that he had no feelings about whatever he had to do for work, but she knew that it was hard on him, firing people or just telling a business that there was no saving it. He would do it, but he would hurt for them too.

How you holding up, love? Smiling, she told Elliot that she was feeling really good about this, but not to tell his brothers. *No, they have big enough heads as it is. I was wondering if, when you're finished there, I could come into town with Cody and we get him some much-needed clothing. He has some that I got him, but nothing for all the time. Then the three of us can get some dinner. What do you think?*

I love it. I have noticed that he wears the same couple of pairs of pants. Did you know that he was washing his own clothes? He said that he knew that. He'd even been throwing in theirs if it was there. *I was going to ask you about getting someone to cook for us. It might be better on Cody if he has a good meal when we can't be there for him.*

I was going to talk to you about that too. And a staff. I don't know about you, but the thought of dusting that house from top to bottom gives me nightmares. When I was living there alone, I would just shut the doors to the other rooms and not think about it. She laughed and felt the others intrude on her conversation. *I have to get back to them.*

All right, my dear, we've talked it over and we can accommodate him. Tell him that we'll give him an extra six months on the payment, and we'll come in and do the hiring for him. Hannah thanked Jason. *No, thank you. I'd much rather give him time than have to dismantle the entire place because he didn't play ball. Thanks for doing this. I hope you know that without you, he would have failed.*

No, I don't think he would have failed, but he'd have given away a part of him that he enjoys to make the payment. He loves those bowls. They're the only thing he's found that he can relax with. I didn't want him to lose that. Jason said that none of them did either. *All right, I'll speak to him and get things set up here with the staff. I think he will need to close down for about a month, then reopen and get people trained. There will have to be a reckoning for the ones that we know are detrimental to the business too.*

Emerald has volunteered to do that. I think we'll just let her be there. She might just kill them when they argue. They all laughed at Grayson when he said that. She made her way to Mr. Peel to talk to him. *Chase is going to do it. Call a meeting for them all, tell them what's going on, then talk to them individually.*

Mr. Peel seemed to be in better spirits when she got to him. He had the small blocks that they were going to use for props for the family, and he had made some just a little bigger at two inches square. Hannah was glad that he was on board with this change. It really would have been a shame to have to kill this plant and fire people.

~~~

Duncan was sitting in the food court of the mall when he saw his kid. It had taken him a couple of minutes to place who he was when he saw him, but that was surely his shit for brains. He wasn't sure what he was going to do to get him back, but watched him with the couple that seemed to be having a good old time. He'd soon nip that shit in the bud.

They were coming out of one of those high-end places with lots of bags when he decided to see about how long they were going to be. When the man left them, taking the bags with him, Duncan decided to make his move. The bitch would be easy to knock around, and he would take his son back.

He could hear them laughing and that, for some reason, pissed him off. Why should he get to have fun when Duncan needed his ass at home? Reaching out to grab Cody, he was down on the floor with his arm up behind his back before he could touch him.

"Mother fuck, bitch, I was just going to take my kid home with me. Let me the fuck go so I can teach you a lesson in touching what don't belong to you." She laughed, and he heard his kid laugh as well. "You won't think this is so funny, shit for brains, when I get done with you."

"And what makes you think he's going anywhere with you? Just so we're clear, he's not. And his name is Cody, not shit for brains. Duncan, I swear to you, you get dumber every time I have the misfortune of seeing you."

"I don't know you." She said that her name was Hannah Crosby. "I know that last name. You're sister to that family? They got money to burn, don't they?"

"I have no idea why you'd think I'd tell you that, but no, I'm not sister to them. I've married one of them. And you do

106

know me, I'm your sister, moron. Julia and I were both at your wedding when you married Rose." He tried to remember, but all he came up with was she was hurting him for no reason. "Rose was sister to Nathan, Julia's ex. You really are stupid, aren't you?"

"I'm no such thing. I just have too much on my mind to think about mundane things like guests at a wedding that happened twenty years ago." She told him it was only ten. "Whatever. Being married to her was like a life sentence."

"As it turned out to be for her. Why did you kill her? Was it because she wanted you to get a job? Did you perhaps decide that you weren't worth the time and effort that you demanded from her? That poor woman didn't deserve anyone like you, and she especially didn't deserve to die like she did." He didn't say anything. He'd gotten off for her murder once; he didn't know whether if he said something now, they'd haul his ass back in. And he knew that was what she was doing. Baiting him so he'd say that he did kill her, and someone was recording it this time. "I'm going to let you go, and you're going to go back to whatever rock you slimed your way out from under."

"You sure are mouthy when you have a man where he can't hit you." She just let him go and stepped back. Duncan didn't reach for Cody again. "Come on home with me, boy. There is a hell of a mess that you left behind for me that you need to get to. I won't put up with you disobeying me. You walk right over here, and I'll not cuff you one for running off."

"No." Duncan was sure that he'd not heard the kid right and asked him what he'd said. "I said no. I'm not going anywhere with you. You killed my mom, and I don't ever want you near me again. I'm in with a good family now, and they love me. In a couple of weeks, they're going to adopt me. As soon as you're in jail. Why don't you go turn yourself in and leave me alone?"

"You can't be adopted by no one when you belong to me. What the fuck sort of things is she telling you that has you believing that shit? You get your ass right here with me, and as I said, I won't hurt you too much." Cody didn't move at all. Not even when the man that had been with them earlier came to stand behind him. "You have no right to my son, mister. And that wife of yours, you need to keep her in line before someone hurts her."

"You think to hurt her?" Duncan said that he was the right man for the job. "Doubtful. But if you'd like to try and take her on, be my guest. She'll mop your ass all over the place. Then I get to take over."

"You'd let your wife defend your honor, or something like that? You're a bigger pussy than I thought you were." The man only smiled and looked at Ann, or whatever her name was. He didn't think it was right that he was to remember family that he hadn't seen in a long time. "I want my kid. If you don't turn him over nicely, then I'm going to call the cops on you."

The woman held out her phone. "Here you go. Use this to call them. I'm sure that they have plenty say to you. Perhaps a few questions too. Like the young boy that was found under your front decking. How about the way you stole from the United States Government by fraudulently receiving aid when you didn't need it?"

"Like anyone cares that my wife got a little extra when I had some money. Big deal." He looked at Cody then. "I heard that she come into some money before she unwittingly got herself murdered. I don't suppose you know where it might be,

108

do you? If so, then you tell me. I want that back."

"You don't deserve anything." His boy was getting very mouthy, and he wanted to slap it right out of him. "You killed her. Taped us both to chairs and put bags over our faces. Mom begged you to let me go, said she'd die for you if you did."

"See? Right there shows you I didn't kill her. She wanted to die." Hannah told him he was a fucking bastard. "Yeah, I might be, but you can't arrest a man without proof. And I think I understood that you can't even bring me in on the murder of my poor wife again either."

Neither of them said a word and he felt a little fear at that. Surely, they would be bragging if they had something on him? The police had stopped going by his old house, and he was glad for that, but he wondered if they were doing something else to find out about the body under the porch. As far as he knew, it was still there where he'd put it. But it mattered little right now — he wanted his kid home.

"You just let him go and I'll take my property home with me." He smiled at them when Cody moved behind the woman. "You think that's going to keep me from getting you, shit for brains? I have news for you; I'm going to get you no matter what they are doing to keep you safe. And there won't be any adopting either. I'm your parent, and by God, you'd better remember that."

"My son is going nowhere with you." Duncan just shook his head at the woman, and told her she was barking up the wrong tree. "Am I? I don't think so. And if you so much as breathe in his general direction, I'm going to make it so you'll have to breathe out of your ass for the rest of your life."

"You sure are a mouthy thing, aren't you? Well, it doesn't

matter. Once you learn whose boss between me and that kid, then you'll be sorry." He didn't even know what he meant by that, and when they laughed at him, he felt his temper rise up. "You keep laughing, bitch, and I'll make it so you're doing it out of the other side of your face."

"That made less sense than the first thing you said. How does one talk out of the other side of their face, I wonder?" She lunged at him, and Duncan fell back over the planter that had been behind him. "Oops, you've fallen down again. I'm to understand that you do that quite often when you're drunk. Come on, guys, we have things to do, and we won't get them done arguing with a fool."

When they turned their backs on him, Duncan stood up. He hated nothing more than when someone was arguing with him and they just turned and walked away. This time when he grabbed for the bitch, he felt himself flying through the air. It wasn't until he hit a wall that he realized that the man, Elliot, had thrown him around like he was nothing more than a speck of dust. He'd not even seen him move.

Duncan sat there on the floor until they were out of sight. He had no idea why, but he thought that they knew just what he was doing and thinking. But that wasn't possible, was it? Limping his way back to his table, he was pissed off that someone had cleared his table of his drink and napkins.

He wasn't happy about a lot of things, and that was just the cake topper as far as he was concerned. But he had more things to do than to sit around the mall and wait on his kid to come back to him. Duncan smiled when he thought how all their hopes of taking the brat from him would be dashed once he got him where he wanted him. He was going to kill shit for brains. Duncan just then decided that.

Going to his car, he was whistling a tune that he'd heard on the radio coming here. He tried to reach Nathan again. The man had been avoiding him since yesterday, and that was pissing him off too. Duncan had questions for the man. Like, did his dead wife cash the check that he'd sent her? Did she know about the house and money before he'd killed her? And had she somehow told the others what was going on? He didn't know. But one thing he did know, he was going to have fun killing off shit for brains. And he would, too, as soon as he got him.

Nathan was on his porch when he got home. There was something off about him, and Duncan decided that he'd keep his distance. When he was about five or so feet from where the other man was sitting, he asked him what he was doing there.

"A vampire came to visit me the other day." Duncan didn't believe in such things and told him so. "Yes, well, you might want to rethink that soon enough. Because he's coming for you too. The whole family is a bunch of vampires."

"So? What does he want with me? And I'm not saying I believe you about them, but what does he want with me?" Nathan stood up and staggered slightly as he made his way toward him. "You just keep your distance, asshole. I don't know what you're on, but you keep away from me."

"His name is Crosby. He's one of the richest men around. Might be the richest man in the world, for all I know and care." Duncan told him to get to the point. "Yes, I'm getting there. He warned me off. Just after he scared me badly enough that I couldn't sleep a wink last night, fearing that he was going to come through my door and kill me. But he did have a message for you."

"Yeah? Well, I don't care. He doesn't scare me." Duncan was on his porch when he remembered that Hannah had said she was married to a Crosby. "What's his first name? This Crosby person. What's his name?"

"Elliot Crosby." Duncan was sure that wasn't the man's name that had tossed him in the mall, but he'd always been bad with names. "He is going to adopt your son once you're convicted of the murder of some kid. Murdering your wife too, I guess. They're working on a case against you, and I'm sure that they'll make it stick this time."

"Why did you come here to tell me this? And for the record, no one is adopting my brat." Nathan said something like if you say so. "He bite you? Or whatever it is that them kind of men are supposed to do to you?"

"Yes, he bit me. Twice. The first time, I didn't know. The second time.... It was a nightmare the things he did to me. Made me see too." He started crying like Duncan's wife had done when he'd knocked her around. "I'm not going to pursue this thing with my wife. She can have it all for all I care. Hell, I'm going to take her the deed to my house today too. I don't want anything to do with her again. It's too dangerous. I will even sign off on the divorce papers, so she can have the kids if she wants them. I don't want to die by that man's hands, let me tell you."

When he was gone, Duncan went into his house. What a fucking pussy the man was. Crying like a little baby about what some man might have done to him. If he really was a vampire, not that he believed in them, then why didn't he just stake him in the heart? That's what he'd do if that happened to him. He was going to gather up some wood and start carving him a nice stake to deal with this asshole. And he was going to stock up on garlic too if he had to. Duncan knew his rights concerning his son and how these people were treating him. He might even sue them for harassing him.

Duncan sat down on the only chair that wasn't blood stained in his living room. This was what he'd come to enjoy the last few days—no one harping on him about shit that he didn't care about. Turning on the television, he tried several stations before he realized that his cable was off.

"Mother fuckers. Why don't they let a man grieve for a bit before they start taking his shit away?" He got up to look for the money. Duncan was going to find it, and he was going to fucking piss on it too. If the bitch wasn't already dead, he'd surely kill her again.

Chapter 8

Packing his things, Nathan didn't think about anything but getting his clothing from the drawers to the suitcase. If he let his mind wander, say to the night of the big Event, as he'd been calling it, he'd die. Just up and die. It was bad enough that he couldn't control his dreams of that night, but during the day, he had to focus on whatever he was doing to keep from just letting his heart stop beating.

He was sure that it had that night. Several times. But he'd kept coming back, his body coming around just as the vampire had told him he would. Nathan was positive that no one had ever begged to die as many times as he had. Looking at the paperwork that he had to mail today, he wondered why no one had ever thought to take his children from him before now. He'd been a horrific father.

The man, Elliot, had shown him what he'd been like to live with. The torture that he'd inflicted on his own family. Even his first wife, the mother of his kids, had been horribly abused by him until she could no longer take it. Killing herself had been her only way out, he realized then. Had she not taken a bullet to her head, then he'd still be beating her up, still hurting the kids, and more than likely would have knocked her up a few more times too. All because he could.

The Event had happened that night, and while he really wanted to think of it as a fluke, that the vampire would never return, he knew better. The entire night, while he was making him suffer in ways that he'd made his family suffer, Elliot had taught him a great many things. Like his abilities were much stronger than Nathan's need to live.

At first it had started out with the life of his children. Not the way that he might have thought, should someone had said that to him. No, this was how they'd been conceived. How they had suffered when he'd beaten their mother while she carried them. Each time he'd hit her during that time, every time he'd been close enough to slap her or knock her to the ground, he'd done so. And the baby that he'd planted had felt every one of them. And as part of the Event, he had too.

Sitting down for a moment, he needed to rest. His body was still hurting. More than that, he was mentally exhausted as well. He could not imagine, nor did he want to again, the pain and suffering that his children had endured. But his wife's — he relived that every time he closed his eyes.

She had been making his breakfast that morning. It had been his favorite. He knew now that she had planned it that way, to try and make amends so that he'd not hurt her again. Little Hayley had been sitting in her high chair, enjoying her breakfast of toast and an egg. It had been all they'd had in the house that he'd not deemed his own food.

This memory was something that he'd never forget, not that he'd be able to. The Event had taken care of that. He would relive her terror of him for the rest of his days. That had been Elliot's plan.

"She suffered with you for so long, and you never had a good word to say to her. The morning of her death, the day that you finally killed her, she tried her best to make you happy, so in turn she could be. But you ruined that, with not just your words, but your actions too." He could see himself sitting at the table, paused in the motion of putting food into his mouth. "See the pain on her face as she stands behind you crying? Do you see how beaten she is? Not just physically, though you did that more than enough to her, but her face. She thought that she had nothing more to live for. Not even for her children."

While he sat there, eating his breakfast of steak and eggs, fluffy biscuits, and fried apples, she was planning the end of her life. There was grits and gravy too. Even a large glass of juice, the pulp all strained out, just the way he liked it. But for his wife and his children, there was only an egg for the baby and toast and water for his other children.

The gun from the cabinet was slipped from the shelf. He could see her now, the way that her face had been set in determination. The way she looked like she had finally grown a backbone. But it wasn't that. She'd not thought of having a backbone, as he had always accused her of not having. It was that she'd finally had enough.

Nathan had been at his parents' home when he received the call. His wife was dead, could he please come and get his children. No, he'd told the cop, he was busy and couldn't be bothered. The cop, he was sure now, was shocked that anyone could have been so cruel.

Kendra, his wife, had cleaned up the kitchen; he could see it all, thanks to the Event. Washing and drying the dishes, she even mopped the floor. One thing that he'd always told her, he would not stand a dirty home. When she'd finished all that she could do, Kendra had bathed their daughter, her chubby little cheeks bruised from him hitting her the night before.

The look in Hayley's eyes was that of lost hope. He never touched his daughter, none of his children unless it was in anger. Nathan had realized during the Event that he'd not seen them much in the later years of living with their mother. She had hidden them away until he had gone away. Not kept them from him, but saved them from him.

After cleaning up the bathing mess, she'd dressed the little girl in the best outfit that she had. It wasn't much. A clean shirt that had seen better days, a sweater that was much too light for the amount of snow on the ground, and two pairs of socks to keep her little feet warm as she took her for the last walk that the two of them would ever share.

Nathan thought of his other children, wondered where they had been that fateful day. He'd never asked. Didn't bother with finding out if they'd been there when she'd gone to their room. All he'd been concerned about was the fact that he was now responsible for his kids and there was no one to feed him. He'd been such a mother fucker then. And he knew that he should have been the one that she killed that day, not herself.

Kendra had taken Hayley to the neighbors. She told them that she had to go away for a little bit, that Nathan would come and get her. They hugged tightly, the child and her, and then she made her way back to the house.

There had been no shoes for her to wear. Nathan had them locked up in the safe, knowing that she'd leave him if she had them. He would have. Long before the day she'd taken her own life.

The room had been prepared, he had noticed when he'd relived the day. Every night and day when he managed to close his eyes, he saw more details that she'd taken care of. The way she had made sure that there was no mess in his home. She had gone to a great deal of trouble to also make it so his kids didn't see what she'd done.

Kendra had wrapped her entire body up in a large sheet of plastic—the kind that was used for windows in the winter months. As she taped the ends closed at her feet and hips, she pulled the phone, the one she'd only been allowed to use in case of an emergency, to her side. Even as she wrapped the plastic over her head and arms, she made the call to the police station.

"My name is Kendra Henry. I live at 127 Maple Street. You must come here soon, I'm going to kill myself, and I'd rather my children not see it." She hung up on the person on the line.

She had been methodical about what she did after that. The gun was lying in her lap, the phone put gently and carefully back on the side table as she prepared herself on the bed. Wrapping the rest of her body in the morbid shroud around her head and face, Kendra put the gun to her head and pulled the trigger.

It was as neat and as clean as that. Called the police, check. Make sure there was no mess for Nathan, check. And then kill herself. She had checked that off before the police arrived to try and save her.

Nathan jumped every time he heard the sound in his head.

119

And he heard it over and over again while he slept or rested his eyes. The Event had shown him not only that he was a horrible person, but that he had indeed murdered his wife. He might not have pulled the trigger, but he had killed her just as surely.

Nathan knew that he should simply end his own life. He deserved it, he knew this. But the vampire told him that if he even thought of such a thing, he'd know and come for him. That alone was what kept him from taking the same gun that had killed his wife and doing the same to himself.

Standing up, he packed the rest of his things. The deed to the house had been signed over to Julia this morning. All he had to do now was put her name on the bank account and leave, never to return.

He also gave her the winning lottery ticket, and a note telling her that he'd used her money to buy it, it only stood to reason that she get it. The divorce papers were signed and filed too, as of this morning. And as of then, she also had full custody of the children. She'd be free to marry whoever she wanted now, hopefully someone that would love her. Julia deserved that more than anyone for putting up with him.

He hadn't done right by her either. But he'd had less time to hurt her in the ways that he had Kendra, and Julia hadn't been as easy to manipulate as his first wife had been. Smiling when he thought of her fighting back, Nathan wondered now why she hadn't just blown his brains out. He wished more than anything that she had.

The house would be sold, he knew that. It had been in his family for a lot of generations. But she had a home, a fresh start too. He only hoped that someday, long into the future, she'd remember what he'd done for her and his kids and think of him once in a while with some kindness. It would be more than he deserved.

Nathan had just enough money to get himself a fresh start. He'd purchased a home, sight unseen, in another state. After he got there he'd furnish it as cheaply as he could and find himself a job. After that, he'd give some of his check each month to the charity that he'd chosen the night of the Event.

"You do realize that you have no right to live, don't you? That you drove someone to their death and you should have to pay for that forever?" Nathan had agreed with Elliot. He'd seen enough in those last few hours to have lasted him a lifetime. "From now on you will be supportive of any charity that helps abused women and children. Volunteer at the shelters, and try your best to make a difference, one that you will give your family now."

"Yes, I can see that now." He had looked up at the big man, terrified out of his mind with what he'd seen and done to him. "I'm sorry. I know those words are hollow now, that I've fucked up more than most, but I am so very sorry for what I've done in my life."

As he left his home for the final time, Nathan knew that he'd been lucky that Elliot had come to him. Luckier still that he'd figured out, too late for some, that he wasn't anyone that people would want to befriend.

Driving away, not even looking in the rearview mirror as he did so, he wondered briefly if Duncan would get the same treatment. And he doubted with all that he was that the other man would ever get it. He was, in a word, fucked.

~~~

"I don't understand." Hannah took the paperwork that had

been handed to her when the two of them went to the bank. The manager had called her sister earlier and asked her to come in. Hannah had been at her house when the call came in and had gone with her. Julia was as confused as she was about what the banker had just told her.

"Your ex-husband, as I'm to understand he is now, decided that everything should go to you and your children, from what I have been told — here, let me see where I put that." While the man looked at his desk, the lawyer for the firm smiled at them. "Yes, here it is. I took the liberty of making sure that you got a copy of the filed deed, as well as the information on the house should you need it."

"But why would he do that?" The attorney cleared his throat and asked if he could have a minute alone with the two of them. The banker clearly as confused as them, said that he'd be outside should they need him. They both turned to him when he started to speak.

"I've called Franklin to come and be here with us while I explain. He's a very good friend of mine, but he was, at one time, one of the best attorneys around." Almost as if he had called him in, Franklin came into the office with Elliot. They sat near them as Mr. Boseman explained more. "I was called in yesterday to go over all this work that was given to the bank to take care of."

He handed the thick file to Franklin, who then spread it out before him on the desk. Hannah had some idea what was in some of the many files, but not enough to tell her sister what she should do. She was glad now that not only was Franklin there, but Elliot too.

"Nathan did all this for his children. Why would he do

that?" No one said a word, and she had an idea that they knew but weren't saying anything. "This isn't what I expected when I was asked to come in here today."

"No, I would imagine not. And had I not been there yesterday when he had all this done, I'm not sure how much longer it would have taken the young man. He was set in what he wanted, and made sure that everything you would need was taken care of so you'd never have to worry." He handed her a sheet of paper from his own file. It was a deed to a home. "This isn't for your children, Ms. Kline. But for you. You may or may not sell the house, though I'm to understand that you are in possession of one now. I'd sell if I were you. and if you don't want the money for whatever reason, I'd set up in a trust for the children."

"The other man, the banker, he said that Nathan has left town and that he's not returning. What happened with that? He wasn't the type of man to just walk away when something he wanted hadn't gone his way." Julia flushed brightly and told Mr. Boseman that she was sorry. "This is, as you can imagine, hard to take in."

"Nathan came in here yesterday morning with not just the deed to the house, but a list of things that he wanted done for you. The money that was in his account, it's been put into your name. The bank just needs you to sign some paperwork. The house is free and clear, and the taxes will be paid from a trust fund that he set up for you as well, if you choose to keep it."

Hannah looked at Elliot when he squeezed her hand. As her sister talked to the attorney with Franklin's help, she asked him what he'd done.

What a thing to say to your mate. Done? Well, what is it you're accusing me of, my dear? It sounds to me like he's had a change of heart and is making amends for his actions. She snorted at him. *You are very lovely when you're confused. Have I told you that lately? And the things that you did to me this morning when I woke —*

Don't you dare try and change the subject. I want to know what you did to Nathan to make him help my sister out after all this time. Elliot smiled at her again, and she found that while she loved him, she could have easily cut his dick off and sewn it to his forehead. *What. Did. You. Do?*

I did pay him a visit. The day before he came here. She asked again what he'd done. *Showed him the error of his ways. Made him realize what he'd done to not just Julia, but to Kendra, his first wife. And what he was continuing to do to his children. Who, I might add, are only as well adjusted for the life they lived because of Julia.*

And did you hurt him? Did you make him do this for Julia? Elliot told her that he had suggested it to him, he'd not made him. *And how did you hurt him? I'm assuming that you did that as well.*

Not much in the physical way, but yes, I did hurt him mentally. Emerald helped me with that, so you know. Hannah waited for him to explain. *The day that Kendra killed herself, the earth was able to feel it when her blood dripped upon the ground. I won't tell you any more than that, like how she did it. But when she was taken from the home, they felt the drop and the pain. And in doing that, Emerald had only to ask the earth what they knew about the woman's last day on earth.*

It was bad, wasn't it? Elliot nodded, and she was glad that he'd not told her what had transpired that day. *So you what — suggested that he turn over all his worldly goods so that she'd forgive him?*

No. And even if she did find it in her heart to do so, Nathan will never forgive himself. That I made sure of until he did what was right by them. She asked him what that meant. *I suggested, and it was merely a suggestion, that he leave Julia better off than she was now. Also, I might have had a hand in him having nightmares until he did.*

And now? The nightmares are gone? So he can go back to being his good old self? Elliot told her that he doubted that Nathan would ever return to his former self. *I'm sorry, I'm being ungrateful about what you did for my sister. But I don't want him to return because he's had a change of heart.*

Elliot kissed the back of her hand. He was holding something back from her. And she had a feeling that he was doing it to protect her. When she asked him if he knew if Nathan would come back, he shook his head no and explained.

As I said, I merely suggested that he make changes in her life. To leave her better off than she had been while married to him. What he did, he did on his own. The lottery ticket that she will receive today, that was unexpected. I thought that he'd take it to use to live on. But he left her that as well. And it's a good deal of money. She asked him where Nathan was. *I know, as I will for the rest of his life, where he is, along with every thought that he has. Should he return, which I highly doubt, I will know that as well. Trust me when I tell you that what I did to him was nothing more than he deserved. The children are now safe, and in full custody of your sister. There is money in the bank for her to care for the children, all of them, including Brett, in the way that they should have been. College will be paid for, and your sister will be happy. Someday, Emerald told me, she will meet her Prince Charming and live happily with her grandchildren and their descendants.*

Emerald said that she'd meet her Prince Charming. Elliot laughed and said that he had paraphrased that part. *I'm sure*

125

that you did. She is a lovely person, but I doubt that she thinks any man other than Chase is Prince Charming.

Her sister was safe. As were her nieces and nephews. The only person that they had to worry with now was Duncan. He wanted Cody in the worse kind of way, and he'd stop at nothing to get him. What he was going to do to the young man terrified her when she thought about it. But he'd never get the chance. Not so long as she had breath in her body.

Julia was set up with the bank. While there a courier came in and delivered an envelope, which contained the lottery ticket as well as a notarized copy of the deed, divorce papers, and the paperwork to give her sister full custody of the children. And he gave her the rights to change their names should they wish. Hannah wasn't sure what that was about, but her sister sat there holding them, sobbing. Her life was about to get so much better, Hannah thought.

Franklin told them that he'd take care of the money from the ticket winnings as well as keeping her name out of the papers. Hannah was glad now that they lived in a state that didn't require you to tell the public that you'd won. There was no telling what sort of monsters that would bring out if the general public knew that Julia Kline Henry was the sole winner of the biggest jackpot ever known.

They had lunch at the local place, and Hannah kept having to remind Julia to eat. She would stare off in the distance not seeing anything, Hannah would bet, with a small smile on her face. Whatever she was thinking, it was making her very happy.

The house, Julia decided, would be sold off. An auction would take care of the pieces that she didn't keep. There were lots of things in the house that she would take for her own, Julia told her. And a great many pictures too. Mostly of the family that her children had come from, and a few of their father. Julia was going to keep some of the things that were clearly from their father's childhood for the kids, things that had been unearthed in the attic by the banker.

"While I don't plan to idolize him in any way, I do want them to know that without his help we'd be in a different situation than we are now." Hannah told her that she was proud of her. "I am as well. And according to Emerald, who terrifies me to no end sometimes, I should be very proud of myself. I didn't let a bully and a prick hold me back from making a good start on my life. She didn't quite say it that nicely, but you understand."

They were both laughing when they exited the little place. There was still a fear around—Duncan needed to be dealt with as well. But with the help of Jewel and the rest of the women, Julia was going to go shopping and buy something for the kids. Besides, she said, Brett's birthday was coming up in a couple of days, and she was going to make it the best that he'd ever had.

Chapter 9

Elliot was working at his desk at home when he felt the hair on the back of his neck dance. Looking up slowly, he reached around the room to find something or anything that might have had his beast on alert. There was nothing there that he could see, but he knew that he was no longer alone on the room.

"I'm not one to fuck with. Whatever you want, it had very well better be worth your life if you don't show yourself." The woman let go of the shadows around her and moved closer to his desk. "That's far enough. What are you doing in a vampire's lair without permission? And again, this had better be good."

"You are Elliot Crosby, son of Franklin Crosby and brothers to the others?" He didn't answer her but felt the probe of her search. He blocked her from that and hurt her in return. "I was only trying to figure out if you were the man that I searched for."

"State your business." He watched her struggle with his magic. "And you still haven't told me how you got into this house."

He knew several things about his visitor. She was young, in terms of a vampire—perhaps only a couple of hundred years old. A virgin, which wasn't really anything that might have bothered him, but for some reason he thought that was important. And she wasn't here of her own will. Someone was forcing her to do this, and he wanted to know why.

"You are Elliot Crosby?" He stood up when she cried out, but watched as a slip of paper fell from her tight fists of pain. When she dropped to her knees in front of him, he not only called his brothers to come to him, but everyone. Whatever was going on, he not only wanted backup, but he wanted help as well.

Someone powerful had sent the girl. To have been able to make her cross over his threshold made him think that it wasn't a vampire, but someone that had some magic of their own. Black, he'd bet—but then, he had no idea. Not touching the girl or the note that she'd dropped, he told her to stand up. Blood poured from her nose and ears as she did what he told her to do.

The first person to enter the room with him was James. And the little faerie was bursting with anger.

"You know her?" James said that he did, yes. "She's someone's puppet. They've sent her here for a reason that I don't know, but it does worry me some."

"Aye, my lord, and so it should." The woman couldn't hear them, he'd made sure of that. And when she struggled again to speak to him, he thought that perhaps she might be trying to warn him of something. He said as much to James. "My lady Emerald is on her way with her dragons. I'm not saying that we will kill the puppet, but it's better to be safe than sorry."

"Yes, I agree." Emerald came into the house as she normally did when something was going on—quietly and full of authority. Ignoring the girl for the note, she had her dragons watch her as they read it over. "It's from her. She wrote this for me."

"And it's in her blood." He looked at Emerald when she said that. Chase and the rest of the family came into the room then. "Whoever did this to her, they meant for you to touch her and be harmed when you did. She is covered in a magic that would kill any other vampire."

The note only said that she had been sent. Not by who or why, but that she had been sent. Elliot was afraid, not for himself—he was an immortal—but for the woman. Whatever was going to happen now, he was sure it wasn't going to bode well for her. He asked Emerald if there was anything they could do to ensure her safety.

"I can do you one better. The fucktard that sent her here, because he touched her to give her this magic, I can summon him forth. If you don't mind." Elliot asked her what that meant. "It could be messy. And by messy, I mean I might have to kill him immediately. I'm going to kill him anyway, but I'd rather get answers first."

He knew as surely as he was standing there that not only would it be messy, but the dragons would do it. He'd seen that happen before, the dragons kill, and thought that he'd rather it not be done in his house. He was explaining this to Emerald just as Hannah joined them.

After bringing her up to date, Hannah went toward the woman. He wasn't sure what she was going to do, but they all waited while Hannah walked around the woman twice before standing in front of her. He wanted to go stand with her, to protect her, when his dad stopped him.

"She's got this." Elliot asked his dad how he knew that. "She's your mate, isn't she? That automatically makes her stronger in my book. Hannah is much tougher than anyone gives her credit for, including herself. Let her do this."

"I'm going to allow you to speak directly to me. All right?" The woman didn't so much as blink. "What's your name? Can you tell me that much?"

"Madison." He looked at Sean when he asked for paper and pen. He started writing things down as soon as Hannah asked her the next question. "No, I cannot tell you who sent me. I am forbidden."

"All right. Good to know. And this forbidden thing, does it hurt you to do what you're not supposed to?" Madison nodded. "I'm going to touch you. I'm assuming that since you were sent here to hurt Elliot that others can touch you. Am I right?"

"I don't know." The scream of pain from the other woman had everyone backing up. "He's telling me to kill all of you."

"He can see us, I'm assuming." Nothing from Madison on that, but Emerald had an idea. She sent one of the small brownies to get the faerie queen, Kilian. Hannah looked at him briefly as she continued talking to Madison. "He's your maker, I think it's called. This man, he made you and rules you."

"Yes." The woman looked directly at Hannah now instead of looking at the floor. The connection to the woman through Hannah made Elliot stagger back slightly on his heels. He had no idea how she had done that, but was willing to search the woman's mind when Hannah asked him to. "You will all die if he has his way."

Madison closed her eyes again just as Kilian entered the room. There was something to calming about her that he was relaxed when she simply came near him. She stood with Hannah when she was told what was going on.

When her name was said, Madison looked at Kilian. "Do you know who and what I am?" Madison said she did. "Then you know that I am more powerful than any being in this world. Even your maker. Do you know that?"

"Yes, my lady, everyone knows that." Kilian reached out to touch Madison and she stepped back. "I don't know if you'll be hurt."

"Nay, child, I will not." Kilian put her hand over the vampire's heart and held it there. "His name is Earl Sams. At least that is what he goes by now. The magic, as you have guessed, is black, but it is paltry to my own. Emerald, if you would be so kind as to bring him to me."

The vampire appeared in the room like he might have been at his own lair. He had been sitting, that was of no doubt, and when he fell on his ass, no one bothered to help him up. But when he did stand, he looked directly at Elliot and cursed loudly.

"Quiet." The man's mouth snapped shut and he looked at Hannah when she spoke again. "Christ almighty man, what the fuck are you going on about? Why are you trying to kill my mate?"

"Mate?" He looked at Elliot then at Hannah again. "You have mated with a whoremonger and a liar. He has cheated me for the last time."

"Really? Well, I'm intrigued as to why you'd think such a

thing. And for the record, you call him anything but Lord Elliot again, and I will send you to hell in a handbasket. Understand me?" He nodded like his head was on a string and it was being pulled up and down. Sitting back on the top of his desk, Elliot was joined there by Ryan. He didn't say anything, but he knew he was working this out too. "Now. We're going to do this quietly and without someone trying to poison anyone. Release the woman to me."

The magic was profound, and Elliot had to hold onto the edge of the desk when it hit him. The woman, Madison, belonged to Hannah. Not him, but to his mate. Looking at his dad, who was smiling like a loon, he had the distinct idea that he was helping Hannah with this.

"You have no right." Hannah said that apparently she did. "You cannot take what is mine. I am her lord and master."

"What sort of fuckery is this? Men wanting to own women? You do know that this is the twenty-first century, and no one owns anyone? And had she really belonged to you, you know as well as I do that I would never have been able to take her from you. Now, sit the fuck down and answer my questions." Earl sat—right where he was standing, he sat on the floor. "In the chair, you moron. Why would you sit there when there is a perfectly good chair right here?"

While Hannah blasted questions at Earl, Elliot reached out for his dad to thank him for guiding Hannah through this so she'd not be hurt. Dad laughed and told him he wasn't doing a damned thing.

Then how is she doing this? I've not made her. She had some of my powers, yes, but I never told her that she could do this to a lesser vampire. His dad laughed again and told him that she obviously didn't need him to show her much about being a vampire. *I can see that. How do you suppose this is working then?*

This is just a guess on my part, but I'd say that she is making it work because the moron in the chair has no idea that she shouldn't be able to. That, my dear son, is what is making this work. She's a good deal braver than any other person I've met, and that is saying a great deal. And I'm sure, before this is over, she'll not only have the answers, but he'll wish he'd never come here.

He looked at Hannah with awe then. She had made a vampire of some age do just what she wanted him to do simply by bluffing. He realized then that he'd never play cards with her. She'd beat his pants off. Which, he thought, wouldn't be so bad. His dad told him to pay attention, Hannah was getting to the good part.

"So you sent a lesser vampire here to kill Elliot simply because, and correct me if I'm wrong, he bought a bit of land over four hundred years ago that you wanted." Earl said that it should have been his. "That's a moot point now, don't you think? I mean, he's owned this land for well over my lifetime, and even that of the little vampire that I took from you. Instead of being a man about it, coming to talk to him and perhaps asking him to sell it to you, you went this route. I don't know, but I think you're about as stupid as stupid comes."

"Stop calling me names." Hannah snapped her fingers and Earl doubled over in apparent pain. "Stop that. You fucking bitch, I'm going to kill you when you set me free."

Hannah laughed. Just threw back her head and laughed hard enough and with enough mirth in it that the rest of them joined her. Then she stopped suddenly, grabbed Earl by the face, and jerked his head around to look at her.

"You have just given me every reason in the world not to ever release you. And since I have shit to do all the time now that I work for the company that my mate owns, I don't have time to babysit a man—a little man that uses women to do his bidding." He shivered, and Elliot knew in that moment that she was going to kill him or have him killed. "Emerald? Remember what you told me about magic and the dragons? Does that apply to morons too?"

"Yes. You have me kill someone that causes you, or is going to cause you or your family harm, and all magic that this person holds belongs to you. So long as it is justified that he did indeed intend to harm." Hannah asked if this was justified. "The queen would be the one to answer that. I cannot. Because as surely as I'm standing here with my dragons at the ready, I would have crisped up his ass as soon as he entered the fucking room."

"Yes, Lady Hannah, you will be justified in your actions. I have no qualms whatsoever in this vampire being put to death." When Earl started to scream and yell about it being unfair, his mouth simply disappeared. Elliot had no idea who had done that, but it bore looking into. If Hannah had, he was going to be much more careful about teasing her. "I would suggest, however, that you do not do so in this room. It's much too lovely to have it tainted by his stain of evilness."

The vampire Earl disappeared. And when Emerald and the dragons did as well, no one bothered to ask where they had gone. Nor did anyone seem to want to follow her. It happened quickly, the death of someone out to harm his family.

Hannah screamed when the magic came to her. He knew that it was happening when Kilian told him not to touch her because he'd only make it worse. There was little he could do to help her with this. She had done this, and she alone would inherit the magic. When she fainted, he asked if he could take her now. Picking her up from the floor, he was stopped by Emerald when she came in the room again.

"She got it all, Elliot." He nodded. "No, I don't think you understand. She got his magic, money, and anything else that he laid claim to. Your mate is not only very wealthy in her own right, but she has several vampires that will only answer to her."

Elliot decided that he'd deal with that later. For now, all he wanted to do was take Hannah to their room and make sure that she was going to be all right. What she had done today — he'd never witnessed a human doing something so brave before. And hoped to never again.

~~~

Franklin could very well have crowed, he was so happy. Christ, she had done it. And all on her own. Hannah Crosby had not just made sure that justice was served, but she also had taken over a kiss. A kiss of terrified and beaten vampires.

He looked at the young woman on the bed and wondered aloud what would happen to them all now. They would need guidance and so much more. Kilian, who had come to check on the young girl, only laughed.

"I don't think there is any way for us to judge what this one is going to do, do you?" He laughed and shook his head. "When Emerald asked me to come to her, I thought I was going to have to kill the man. I've done it before, vampires that thought themselves above such laws as were set before them. But imagine my surprise when our young human not only did what needed to be done, but she also did it without help from any of us."

"Elliot thought that I was doing it, telling her what to say. I wish could have taken credit, but this was all her. I'm glad that I got to witness such a thing. I would never have believed it otherwise." Kilian said that she was glad too. "I can feel her magic now. Can you?"

"Oh yes, she got a great deal from this. And as soon as the dark magic came to her, she was able to change it to white. That is another thing I would like to know about her. Where did she get such knowledge?"

They both stood when Hannah sat up in the bed and looked at them. "I can hear a fucking fly farting in the wind. Is that normal?" Kilian said it was. "Then how the fuck do I stop it? There are just things that I do not want to hear. Did you know that when deer mate, they make this whining noise? I do now. And I don't care for it."

Hannah swung her legs over the side of the bed and put her head between her knees. He was worried about her, wondering if she was all right, when she started talking again. Franklin asked her to repeat what she had said, and she sat up.

"I said that there are all these memories racing around in my head that I didn't make. Is it Earl?" Franklin told her that he had no idea how that worked. "Yeah, me either. And for the record, I'm a researcher. I did my homework as soon as I found out that I would be living with a bunch of vampires. There isn't much out there, but enough to make me go to someone for answers."

"Emerald." Hannah said partly, but not all. "You've been a very busy girl, I think. And I, for one, am proud to have you as a member of his family."

138

"You might not think so when you have to help me run a kiss." He asked her why him. "Because, while your sons are highly respected and loved, you are the man that people go to when they need something. For a great many years you have been helping people, vampires and humans alike, that even your boys don't know about."

"Who told you that?" She said again that she was good at researching. "You won't tell on an old man, will you?"

"When I find this old man, I'll let you know." Hannah stood up and stretched. He saw it then — Franklin saw that she had become a vampire with all this. The magic of being one was all around her. When she looked at him with a wink, he was sure that she'd been aware that could happen too. Christ, he loved this young girl. "I was wondering if you could call a meeting for me. I'd like for the pack master to be there, as well as his second. We have to warn them about what has happened to their realm, as well as this one. Not bad, but it might change things around here and I don't want anyone hurt."

When Hannah said that she was taking a shower, both he and Kilian left the room. Elliot was just coming up the stairs with a tray of food, and Franklin realized that Hannah had spoken to him too. These two, they were going to be something when this all came together. And he was glad, with all his heart, that Kilian had done what she'd done for all of them all those years ago.

He reached out for his sons to tell them first that Hannah was awake, then how she'd come to have those answers. Chase was laughing so hard at that, Franklin had to wait on him before he could tell him that there was going to be a meeting.

You do know what this is for, don't you Dad? He asked Sean what he knew. *She's going to share with us. Whatever she got, she's going to give us some of it. And while I think that's really nice of her, I'm not going to take it. I want her to have it.*

Why? I mean, why would you turn it down, son? Not that I'm upset, but what makes you think that you don't need it? He explained to his dad. *She already said that I was going to help her run the kiss. I don't know that she'll need me much, but I think she could keep them in line without all of it, don't you?*

I don't know, that's the point. I won't be able to live with myself if something happens to her because her magic was depleted. It was a sound argument, but Franklin didn't know how that was going to fly with her. She was pretty determined and told him that. *Yes, well, so am I. And I'm much older.*

For some reason Franklin didn't believe that was worth a hill of beans. She'd not had a lick of magic when she'd dealt with Earl and look at what she'd done. No, he didn't think she'd let them get by with that excuse. But he was going to be front row and center when he tried.

"Do you suppose that when she takes over the kiss with you, that they'll be accepting of her?" Franklin asked Kilian what she meant; did they mean to hurt her? "The only thing I know for certain is that they're starved, and they're in a place in their mind that might not be a good thing for the young woman. She'll need to help them before she can guide them."

"I don't even know where this kiss is. I'm assuming that it's not far from here. Being that the young woman said she'd walk to her place." Kilian told Franklin that Madison hadn't gone to the kiss, but to her actual home. "And why does she have so much when the others do not? I'm not trying to cause trouble here, but why does she?"

"The house, as she calls it, is nothing more than a couple of walls around a stone floor. She lived in the mountains when she could get away." Franklin felt terrible for his words. "You would not have known otherwise, Franklin. But the kiss isn't far from here. It is in the next town over, and secluded in where it sits. But it is nothing more than a few boards thrown together to make a place for them to hide during the day."

He thought about that, how rich his family's lives were because they'd been smart. Not always, but smart in life choices and when it came to money. Franklin wondered how the town would fare if they were to release these vampires to the world.

"How many are there? This kiss? Not many, I would bet." She told him that she had felt four that were still living. "He's killed some of them. In anger?"

"Yes. He was not a man who took things as they came. His anger was violent and painful to those that served him. Several of them have taken their own lives by meeting the sun so that they could be free." Franklin hurt for that. To end a live so tragically. It was what he had once planned, but no more — he wasn't going to do that. "Franklin, what are you thinking?"

He didn't get a chance to answer her, but his mind was working on it. Hannah and Elliot came into the room, and they both seemed to glow with happiness. They were in love, as it should have been, but he had a feeling that it was more than that between these two. There was a shared trust as well. Strong enough that they could and would take care of the kiss.

The meeting was called to order, and Cody joined them when the food was spread out on the table. His grandson, he just then realized. Cody was his very first grandchild, and he could not have been happier. Sitting next to him at the table, he tried to think how to brooch the subject of asking him if he'd call him Grandda. But when he looked at him, he could see the touch of makeup or something that he'd used to cover up something on his face. Anger, unlike he'd ever felt before, surged forward, and it was all he could do not to scare him.

"Do they know? Your parents, do they know you've been hurt?" Cody shook his head, then put it down again. "Who was it, son? I'm asking you because I want to know who I have to kill who dared harm my grandson."

"Do you want me as your grandson, Mr. Franklin?" He told Cody that he'd be honored to be his grandda. "I've been meaning to ask everyone what I was to them. You have no idea how happy you've made me right now."

"I'm glad I could help." Cody looked around the room. Franklin was sure that any one of them could hear the conversation that was going on between them, but he kept his voice low all the same. "Who was it?"

"My dad. He found me, and I only just got away. I was afraid that he had me for sure. But I hurt him too, so you know." Franklin nodded and looked at Elliot. He had heard. Franklin would bet any amount of money that at this moment, his son was planning the murder of Duncan Wayne, and he would be a dead man before too much longer. And he would suffer too. "You're not going to tell them, are you? They're so happy right now, and I don't want that to be messed up."

"You don't worry none about that. They're just as happy as a singing bird in summer that you're their son." Elliot nodded once and looked at Grayson, who he'd been talking to. "Yes, sir, you have nothing to worry about on that score."

Chapter 10

"I did nothing. I had no power at all." She was sure that no one believed her, so Hannah tried to think of the best way to explain to them what she'd done to Earl. "Look, when you go into a business that is failing or close to it, you talk to them by pulling no punches at all. Tell them like it is. Correct?"

"Yes, but what you did was different." She asked Grayson what she had done. "You made him do things that he'd only have done if you had compulsion and mind control. You're trying to tell us that you had neither. You did."

"No, I didn't. I'm just that good." Frustrated, she asked Chase, the most laid back of the men, to stand. He was smiling at her, and she loved this man. But she had to start with someone. "I want you to clear your mind of everything but me."

He looked at Elliot. These men were wonderful, but they had this crazy unspoken rule to never touch, never think about nor touch the others' mates. She knew that she'd thought of the never touch thing twice, but it was a biggy to them. Crazy rules.

Also, kind of sweet.

"Hmm. I don't think I'd like to do that. It might get me killed on all kinds of levels. You might want to pick someone else." Beyond frustrated now, she ordered him to sit. When he did, it took him several seconds to realize what she'd done. "You didn't use compulsion."

"That's what I've been trying to tell you, fucktard. All I did was make you think that I would harm you if you didn't do what I told you. You knew that I wouldn't harm you, yet you sat because some tiny part of you was worried that I could. It's the same with Earl. I made him believe that I had this power over him by my tone, my stance, and actions. It was the packaging that he was afraid of, not me. He might not have done it had I been all shy and reserved before stepping up to the plate. Emerald uses it too, but the difference is, people knowing what she is already colors what they think."

"And you use this when you are working with someone on the front line. You made them aware of what?" She told Franklin. "You made them think that you had every answer? Well, I'm guessing that it worked. And worked well. Did you know that your old firm is now looking for you? They want you back in the worse sort of way, my dear."

"Figures. No one really did the research. They would skim over details, see if there were loopholes in something, and that would be the end of it. Me, I like to know it all. From the date that the concept of the business came to light all the way to how they might ship out the product that they want to produce. I would know names, shipping companies that would be able to handle their business. I left nothing unsearched, and it paid off for me." Sean asked her if she had used it with all businesses.

"No, sadly, some of them are just going to fail simply because they have it in their head that they're going to. It's the same concept, but worked in the opposite way. You understand."

"Yes, I think we do." Chase sat down after pacing the entire length of the room twice. "Remind me to never play any sort of mind games with you. I think you'd have me believing that I'm going to have our baby. By the way everyone, Emerald is going to have a baby in seven months."

Everyone congratulated the happy couple. She hugged first Emerald then Chase, because she could. It was funny how they did things in this family. She supposed it was because they were very old, and while not set in their ways, they did have rules that they'd always followed. Hannah stood next to Elliot as the rest of the family got settled again. Then Grayson turned to her with the oddest smile.

"I have a question for you. And you can answer or not, but do you know what sort of magic you have now? I mean, can you do anything different than before?" He laughed and looked around the room. "I don't know about you guys, but the way she handled Earl makes me think that the magic that she got is going to benefit us all."

"I've not really played around with it. Not even the stuff that Elliot told me that I have from being his mate. But the magic that I was able to share with all of you, it wasn't all that much, I think. Elliot said that you got a little zap but nothing that hurt. I'm to understand there is a lot for being the mate of one of you guys." They all nodded and told her a few of the things. "Dressing without having to think about what to wear sounds perfect for me."

There was also the immortality thing that scared her a little.

She understood the concept of it, and living forever with Elliot sounded great. But she wasn't like any of these guys. She was just a plain Jane that had no prior magic inside of her. Did she get older? Did they change at any point from what they looked like now? She knew other vampires and what their immortality was, but she had been told that theirs was much different. This family could never be killed, not by a stake to the heart or even trying to remove their heads. Hannah wondered how that worked.

When dinner was called, she realized that she was starving. But mostly she was extremely thirsty. Not just for tea, which was her usual thing to drink, without lemon or sugar, but today she wanted juice. A lot of it too.

Their new cook seemed to have a grasp on what she needed faster than she could tell him. Sitting by her plate was a large glass of mango juice, and she nearly drained it before setting it down. The glass simply filled to the rim again, without the aid of a bottle or pitcher. She looked at Ryan when he laughed.

"You did that." She shook her head. "I'm pretty sure that you did. We can do that too, but not as easily as you did it just now. I'd have to touch the glass or even you to fill it with juice. And I'm sure that whatever is in the glass, it's something that you love as well. I would have put orange juice in the glass."

Picking up the glass again, she thought about her favorite juice. When the glass of liquid changed from a pretty shade of yellow to a dark red color, she sipped what she thought of as the nectar of the gods. It was cherry and lime juice.

"I have another question for you if you are finished having fun with your glass." When she looked at Emerald and she winked back at her, Hannah smiled. It was hard to know when she was kidding or not. But she did like the other woman. "Can you apply this non-magic that you do to humans as well? I don't know if you were aware of this or not, but the business that you're helping, he's a tiger. Not human at all."

"Yes. Though I have to tell you, I'd never used it on a non-human before. And I can tell the difference, too. I think that stems from something my dad taught us a long time ago how to tell humans from others. It's not foolproof, but it works about ninety percent of the time." Emerald asked her what the tells were. "Well, they move in a graceful sort of artform. Not that humans don't, but a shifter, for example, moves like they are not only aware of their body and their other half's, but like they can change into the other being without much effort. Again, I think that would be confidence. Also, they tend to move faster. Not just walking, but when something is going to happen that they can get to or out of the way from."

"Those are good tells, and ones that I try very hard not to use when I'm around the public. I'm sure that I have a few, but for the most part, I can blend in well with the population." Hannah looked at Jason when he spoke again. "I'm guessing that you have an idea that I have tells."

"You do. All of us do for one thing or another. Let's take Emerald. She's the scariest person I know, human or otherwise. But even she has them." Emerald asked her what they were. "If I tell you, you have to teach me how to use a sword. It's been a longtime passion of mine to learn that particular dance."

"All right, I can do that. But you learn with the idea to kill or be killed. All right?" Hannah said that she'd not have it any other way. "Good. What do you think I do to make it known that I'm not human?"

Instead of answering her, she walked to her and put her hand out. When she easily put her hand into hers, Hannah squeezed it. The returning squeeze nearly put her to the floor, but Emerald smiled as she let her go. Then she asked her what else.

"You tap your foot when you're nervous. Not a lot, but just tapping. And when you're about to kill someone, you shift. Just enough to let a bystander know that they should back off. Also, you play with your fingers, making steeples out of them, when you don't believe a word out of the person you might be speaking to." Emerald nodded, and Hannah knew that she'd never see those traits again. She decided to keep the last one to herself, how she played with her hair when she was embarrassed. "Chase isn't hard to read at all. He has this tell that gives him away quickly. The way you look at a person, deep and probing. No one stares a person in the eye as much as you do. It makes even the most comfortable person not so much anymore."

"And this is a tell. What is it? Like the others, I'd like for people that I don't know that well not be able to tell what I am. At least until it's too late." She walked up to Chase and stood behind him when she asked him to look in the mirror. She knew that he could see himself there, not his human form but the vampire beast beyond that. "Christ, I had no idea. He's right there, my other part of me."

"Yes. And for some reason, you're the only one whose beast I can see. The others have tells as well—hardly noticeable, but we all have them." Jason asked her what hers was. "It's easy once you know about it. I know that I have it, but I can't seem to stop myself from playing with anything that is in front of me.

148

A pen, I'll play with that. Paper, I shred that up into tiny pieces. If there is food around, I simply crush it until it's nothing more than dust. It's why I don't have anything in my hands when I'm talking to a person I'm trying to help."

They all talked about what they thought the others might have. For the most part, they were all correct. But she doubted that any of them would be able to tell them all. It had taken her a long time to learn to find them. and it had paid off well for her.

When supper was called, they all entered the dining room. It was a family affair, something that she was sure that they'd done since they had figured out that they could eat food. They loved each other, and the thing about that was, they didn't have any trouble showing it. When it came to protecting one another, she knew that they'd do it for the other to the death too. This family had seen a lot of changes in the world, but, to her anyway, she didn't see where it had jaded them too much.

"You did very well in there." She kissed Elliot when he did her. "I have a request, however. When they all leave, I'd very much like for you to be naked in our bed waiting for me. That way I can show you my tells so you know that I want you."

"You want me all the time." He wiggled his brows at her and she had to laugh. "You are such a goofball, and I love you more every day."

~~~

Duncan nursed his hand and wondered where the hell that boy got off fighting back like he had. Sure, he'd hit him a few times, but that had been his job as his father. To keep him in line and doing what he'd told him to do. His mother never learned that and look where it got her. Dead as a doornail.

149

There was a long scratch on the top of his hand. But that's not what bothered him. It was the bruise that was forming on his palm. The kid had actually hit him with a hammer when he'd tried to grab him. What the hell was he thinking he was going to do? Kill him?

"Not fucking likely." Duncan knew that he was bigger than his son, but the brat was faster and lighter on his feet. When he'd grabbed for shit for brains, he'd never in his wildest dreams ever thought that he'd fight back. Not only had he fought back and fucking won this round, but he'd injured him in the process. "Someone is going to regret teaching that kid it was all right for him to hurt me."

Duncan wandered around his house. Not the one that he'd lived in with Rose, but the one that he had from his childhood. He'd never noticed how out of date the place was until he had his own place. Well, his wife had had her own place. He missed her in times like this. Duncan could have cooked himself something to eat, but his culinary skills were limited to grilled cheese and a bowl of cereal. And even the grilled cheese would be iffy. Sometimes he'd get caught up in something and forget about it. Then he'd have grilled tar-tar sandwich.

The house that he'd shared with Rose had been government property. They had given her the little house when he'd been out of work and not paying her money. She had them a place to stay and somewhere he could go for a quick meal, a good fuck, and a bed to sleep in. The fucking wasn't all that good—he'd have to fight her for it—but in the end, like in all things, he won out. Then his kid had hit him.

He'd gotten in a few punches of his own when he'd had him down once. But the kid was a lot stronger than he remembered him to be. He wondered if it was because shit for brains was eating better. He'd seen the amount of groceries that went into that house. As if they were feeding several armies.

Cody had also been wearing really nice clothes, like the kind that someone had went and bought for him rather than just getting something off the free clothing drive. Not that he didn't have nicer clothing too, but his kid seemed to be wearing them a good deal better than he had any of his things.

Duncan knew that he'd turned into a fat slob. Even his shirts, the kind he used to make fun of people having to wear, were actually a little too tight on him. And when he tried to do something more than shovel more food into his mouth, he'd be so winded that he'd have to sit for a spell. That was not the way that he wanted to be right now. Being lazy was one thing, but being fat and lazy was something that he'd sort of worked to not happen all his life.

His mom had been fat. And a slob. She told him it wasn't her fault, but he knew better. She really didn't eat all that much, not that there was much growing up, but she'd save what she could for him. That was until his stepfather had come along and started telling him how things were going to be.

It had taken him a little while to understand that the man was staying, no matter what he did. Knocking around his mom had seemed, even to him, to be a good time for the old man. And he'd taught Duncan that a woman should know her place, and that place was either under him or fixing him something to eat. Again, it wasn't until he was older that he understood the first part, but he'd gotten it. Then he'd found a wife that he could do the same thing to. But the kid had come around.

He'd hated him from the start. All he did was cry, whine,

and want something from his mom. There was late dinners after the brat had squirted himself into the world, as well as laundry not done and the house a fucking mess with toys and shit when he got older.

Duncan had also noticed that the kid would avoid him when he could. At first Duncan had figured that his mom was doing that, telling him to run and hide. But after she was gone he'd done it on his own. That was how he'd come up missing after she'd been murdered.

He wasn't delusional enough to think that what he'd done to Rose was anything but murder. He'd killed her straight out, and would do it again if he could. She had been trouble, and more than that, she was pretty useless to him when it came to getting shit for him.

Like the food card. He knew that she had it, and while he'd never gone to the store with her to use it, there was things that he wanted her to get for just him. Pretty much anything that was expensive, he supposed. And he didn't care for her and the kid forever taking food out of his mouth, so to speak. Killing her off, that had been a blast. But he still had no way of using the fucking card. There wasn't any code number that he could find so he could swipe it in one of those readout things.

Tomorrow he had an appointment with a social worker. He was going to get his kid back to where he belonged, as well as a new number on that card. Duncan was tired of having nothing to eat all the time. And the kid was going to be cooking it for him, not being adopted out by a family that had more money than sense.

Duncan had thought about selling him to the Crosbys, but that wouldn't have worked. They were all law-abiding people, and selling kids...he knew as well as anyone that would get you big time in prison. No, he'd just keep an eye out for his kid, but be more careful this time.

The brat had been coming out of the library of all places. Why did he need to go there? He couldn't eat in the building, he knew that, nor could he just hang around. Once when Rose was recovering from one of his lessons, he'd went to the place to find out how to set her bone. The leg had never been right after that.

Rose hadn't been in the best of moods when she was hurt or upset. The few times that she'd had to go to the hospital, he'd refused to take her. They asked questions, and Rose would never lie for him. She'd end up at the hospital because she'd send the kid off to get a neighbor or something and they'd take her lazy ass in. He'd never given her a phone, nor was there one in the house. But she always managed to stay one step ahead of him when she needed something.

He thought of the day that he'd killed her. He'd gotten up late, and he noticed that there was a lot of noise in the house. Laughter and such. It hadn't woken him up, but when he heard it, he had been irritated. He'd never know what had set him off — the fact that his son was home or that she was giving him something to eat. The boy should have been getting his own food and not taking his. He didn't know, but whatever it was, it ate at him like he had a worm in his gut.

"What the fuck are you doing?" She turned and looked at him, anger in her eyes, and she had the butcher knife too. "You put that away, or so help me, I'm going to make you regret living."

She said something; he was never sure whether she was

telling him she did anyway or for Cody to run. But it mattered little. He grabbed hold of the kid as he was darting by him and jerked the knife from his mother.

Rage consumed him, it seemed like. Stabbing Rose in the belly, he watched as she fell to the floor. He cuffed the kid in the head then, and got to work making them both pay for their behavior.

Rose hadn't been easy to get in the chair. She was slick now with all the blood, and she wasn't the least bit helpful. It was like working with slippery dough to make bread. Just kept squirting out all the time. By the time he got her tied up, he was exhausted. But he had to make them both pay for this, and began to tie his son up as well. It hadn't occurred to him to kill either of them. He was going to hurt them both a great deal, but not kill them.

But as soon as she woke up she started screaming her fool head off, and he put the plastic bag over her face to shut her up. He watched in fascination when the bag tightened and then let go as she breathed. Yes, that was when he decided to do it. Rose was going to die anyway, and having the kid see it would be epic. It would scare the shit for brains into doing what he told him to do.

Duncan had made it last as long as he could. Taking the bag off her face and letting her breathe again. But she was getting weaker all the time, and he wished even now that he'd not stabbed her first. He might well have had a week or more of doing that to her.

But the boy hadn't heeled for him. Instead, he got mouthier and ran off more. Not that the latter had bothered him too much, but he had wanted a hot meal on the table when he got home from his day and the brat would not do it. Beating him didn't work, and it had lost its appeal when he stopped crying when he'd hit him. Just looked at him with the same color eyes that he had, and it had creeped him out a little.

Then one day the people from the school had come by just as he was getting home. An all-nighter of playing cards and drinking hadn't left him in the best of moods, and he might have been all right had he not threatened them.

He had to produce his son for them. Duncan might have told them that he didn't know where the boy was since his mother took off. Neither of them said anything, the woman looking around, the man just staring hard at him. "My wife, she's ran off, and I think that sh—Cody is acting out because he misses her so much."

Duncan didn't think it would do him much good to call his son shit for brains either. He was glad that he'd caught himself on that one. And he really didn't have a clue where the kid had gone off to. Hopefully he'd fallen in the river behind their house and was right now fish food.

But he'd not be that lucky. The kid was probably waiting for them to leave his house so that he could flag them down and spill the beans about what he'd done. And just lately he'd noticed the smell coming from the porch. Damn it, he'd hoped it would stay frozen until he could bury it someplace.

Now he had one week to bring Cody in and let them talk to him. Apparently, his grades had slipped a little. Duncan had been thinking that they'd meant he was getting all failures, but they said that he'd gone from an A in all his classes to an A-. He had just stared at them when they had said that.

"But he's getting good grades. Probably better than most,

I'm guessing." The woman, he could not remember her name for the life of him, said that Cody was already taking advanced math and English. "Then why the fuck are you bothering me about his grades? Hell, lady, it sounds like he's smarter than any of you."

And now, because Cody had not been able to hold his tongue, he was to bring Cody to their offices and leave him with them until they said otherwise. There were things he had to answer, and things they wanted to say to him. Duncan was afraid that what they wanted and what they got were going to land him in prison. For a very long time.

So, he had a plan. It was brilliant, yet also scary. Not for him, not really. He was going to snuff out the kid and make it look like he'd not been able to live without his mom anymore and had killed himself. He'd read up on it, and the grief would be horrible for someone so young, and they suggested that he be watched for signs of depression and such. Shit for brains was playing right into his hands. As soon as he found him, that was. He was getting good at hiding from him. But Duncan knew that his luck would change soon. And when it did, he was going to take care that no one could prove that he'd killed his mom.

"Fucking little shit. Doesn't he know I have things to do?"

He stomped through the grocery store looking for something to have for dinner. He had no idea how to cook himself a meal, but he figured that if Rose could do it, then there shouldn't be any trouble for him to do it.

But there were too many choices to be made. Turkey and dressing. Meat loaf. There was fried chicken that he could make, and they even came with a bit of dessert too. Grabbing about half a dozen of them, he made his way to the front.

He was going to have to pay cash for his meals, he only just remembered, on account'a Rose had done such a good job of hiding that stupid government card from him. This shit was stupid too. And someone was going to pay. He hoped it was Cody. That kid had been a pain in his side since he slipped out of his mother's body. Fucking kids. Well, he was going to rid the world of one of them as soon as possible.

Chapter 11

As soon as the last person was out the door, Elliot grabbed Hannah and nearly tossed her to the wall. He was needy, more than she was, and she could see his beast there. Waiting. It seemed to her that he was always waiting on something.

"You're way too dressed for what I have in mind." When he stopped suddenly and lifted his head from her neck, she tensed up too. "We're about to have company. It seems our new cook has some questions for us."

"Let's run upstairs. You do that really quick trot thing you do and take us up to our room." His grin was lecherous, and she shivered the length of her body. Before she could ask him what he was thinking, they were in their room and she was pressed against the door.

His hands were everywhere. She realized at one point that she was naked, and moaned when his mouth seemed to follow his hands. When he was down on his knees in front of her, she stared at him with rapt fascination.

"Your eyes are blood red." He said that he could only see her in a haze, and his words were slightly slurred. That was when she noticed that his fangs were incredibly long and lethal looking. "Are you going to bite me?"

"Oh yes, I am." He licked along her inner thigh before looking up at her again. "Come for me, my love. I want to drink your nectar and feed from you."

He pulled her body to his mouth. She waited for him to bite her, to sink his teeth deep into her, but all he did was pause, watching her. Before she could ask him what was going on, he licked her womanhood and she cried out with it. It felt delicious and amazing. And that was the last coherent thought that she had.

He ate her pussy like he had never had a meal before and was filling up on her. Hannah cried out so many times, clinging to the wall while he feasted upon her. Even begging him was no use. Elliot made her weak, and she was sure that was his plan. Then she felt his teeth graze over her thigh and excitement coursed through her.

Elliot never took his eyes off hers as he leaned down and licked her pussy. She could feel the difference right away. Whatever he'd done, she could swear he'd warmed her up from the inside out. And then when he pulled her closer to him, his mouth right there, he bit her hard and she screamed. Not from pain, though there was a lot of it, but from her release. She clawed at the wall behind her and felt the paper under her nails give. It was carnal, the way that she came, and savage. Pulling his head from her, she nearly came again when Elliot licked the bit of blood on his lip.

She was suddenly lifted up, and her back touched the bed

before she could wrap her arms around Elliot. But he was there for her, his body poised over her, his cock seemingly stretched to take her. Reaching down, Hannah wrapped her hand around him and he moaned.

"You do that and I'm not going to be able to finish what I've started." She fisted him up and down, using the precum that dripped from the tip to do it. When he started to fuck her hand, she sat up slightly, but he pushed her back to the bed. "It's my turn."

She knew that he was going to take her, and he did. But it wasn't like before, where they made love gently. He was hard and took her the same way. When she wrapped her legs up and over his, he took her faster, harder than before. And when he nuzzled her neck, she knew that when he bit her, she was going to have a climax like never before. Giving him what he wanted, she turned her head and let him see that she was willing to give him her all. Her own teeth seemed to stretch and grow. She knew then that she had fangs, and that she could bite him as well. And when he bit her, everything that she could have imagined, hoped for, or even been told about paled in comparison to being with this man. Sinking her teeth into his flesh gave her so much more than she ever imagined. And the way his blood seemed to fill her in a way that nothing else had, she knew that she was in love, more so than just an hour ago.

Hannah woke up sometime later. She knew that it was late — the room was dark with it and there wasn't a sound in the house. Elliot was sleeping next to her, and she thought about snuggling up to him but decided instead to get up. After dressing, she made her way down the stairs and to the living room, the one room that she loved more than any other.

161

Sitting in the large room — the lights off and there wasn't a sound — she thought about being here, with this man, and how she'd gotten here. Her sister had needed her. And if she'd tried to do it on her own as Julia would do at times, she would never have met the man of her heart.

Not her dreams — she wouldn't have been able to dream of such a man, but her heart had needed him and there he was for her. And to think that she'd been so hard on him when she'd first seen him. Smiling to herself, she thought that it might have been good for them both, for her to be a bitch.

She must have dozed off at some point because she woke to Elliot saying her name. He was dressed up, and she asked him what was going on. Stretching her arms over her head, she heard him growl and laughed at him.

"I'm very worn out. You did this to me." He grinned like a little boy. "So, you didn't answer me. Where are you headed?"

"I have some things to do for the family, and that requires me to go out of town for the day. Not that long, but to drive to Columbus and back takes longer because of the traffic. I'm to understand that you have an undertaking today too." She was confused for a moment, then thought about her plans. "My dad is looking forward to watching you at work. He said it was going to make his day watching you take care of Mr. Allen. The man has been a burr up our ass for a decade or more."

She was supposed to meet Franklin at the shop at ten. It was just after eight now, and she still had to read the rest of the reports that she'd found out. The man was dirty — there was no way that he was going to be able to tell her any differently. Not that what he did with his own money was any of her concern, but what did get her panties in a twist was that he was using

162

company funds to pay off his bad debts. And that was hurting them in the long run.

By the time she was ready to go, she had all her notes in a row. Some of the things that she'd unearthed were stuff she was sure he thought was buried. But with her talent, she supposed, she'd not only been able to find it, but also to figure out what had happened as an end result of it. When Franklin met her in the front offices of the building, he hugged her tightly.

The man in question in all this, Ethan Allen, was sitting at a long table that she thought was a little over the top. There were two men with him—she assumed they were attorneys, and wondered what was going on. Looking at Franklin gave her an idea that he knew and was loving it. Hannah sat down and pulled out the first of many things she wanted to talk about.

"Before you begin, I'd like for you to meet my sons. This is Ethan Junior and my youngest son, Daniel. They would like to go over a few things on their own, if you don't mind." She did mind and said as much. "Well, since you've had me carve out a portion of my day for you to tell me whatever you have, then you will listen to me."

She'd had enough. The man wasn't going to budge, so she did the only thing that she could do. Hannah stood up and started putting her things away. Franklin just sat there, and she didn't even bother looking at him when she did Mr. Allen.

"In three days you're going to be closed up. With the deadlines to payroll coming up, the taxes that you're behind in, as well as the balloon payments at three different banks that are due next week, you're not going to be able to survive this." Daniel asked her about the banks. "Didn't he tell you? In addition to coming to our firm for money, he has secured three different loans from banks across the United States. All of them thinking that if they have to—no, let me rephrase that. When they have to foreclose on this venture, they'll get the business as well as the property that it sits on. Which you do not own."

"No, you must be mistaken. Dad would have told us that." Daniel looked at his father, and Hannah knew the exact moment that he realized that he'd been lied to. "What else have you been able to find out, Mrs. Crosby? At this point I've had about enough of the shit going on here."

"Are you actually taking her side over mine?" Daniel said that apparently her side was the one that was telling the truth. "You don't need to know every little detail about this business right now, Daniel. When I die, that's when you can make decisions for it."

"From what she's told us, when you do pass away, then there will be nothing left for us anyway. She said within the week. You told Ethan and I that you were having a little blip in your financial needs." He looked at her as his father went on about loyalty and ungrateful children. "Do you have anything that can prove this is what is going on? Or is this all supposition on your part?"

She didn't take offense at his questions. It was more than likely something that she'd have done too. But she handed him the paperwork on not just his tax returns that were made public record, but copies of his bank statement for the last several months. There was a statement on what should have been his tax payments as well. All of them in the red except his personal bank statement. Hannah was really glad that no one asked her how she'd gotten them.

He looked each of them over as his dad still talked about

how he was betraying his family. When he turned to his dad, or brother, she wasn't sure, Hannah could almost feel sorry for the man.

"The company is done." He handed everything to his brother and leaned back in the chair. "You knew this before coming here. That we were going to have to close up. Why did you even take this meeting if you knew that?" She handed him the paperwork that Jason and Chase had given her last night. It was an attempt to save not just the company, but the jobs there as well. As he read it over, she watched Ethan and his dad argue.

They looked alike, the two of them. but she'd bet anything that was where the sameness ended. Ethan, the younger, was the smarter of the two of them as well. And she'd bet anything that when he saw the stipulation in the paperwork given to them, he'd gladly fire his father and take over the business with his brother.

When Daniel was finished, like before he handed the paperwork to his brother. Mr. Allen tried to take it from him, but Ethan told him to sit down and be quiet. It was telling in that moment that the sons would try their best to make this work.

"This proposal, it's nonnegotiable, correct?" She told him it was set in stone on how they would help them out. "And if we don't do this—I'm not saying that we won't—but what will your firm do then? It seems to me that they're losing more than we are if nothing happens."

Franklin cleared his throat before he spoke. "There are four firms that we have been talking to that will take over the production here. Men that are willing to go the extra mile in making this place viable again. People who have no need to steal from the ones that work for them, nor place the blame on others." Daniel asked him how long he'd known this was going on. "I would say from the beginning. It was only recently that Hannah found out that he was neglecting to pay it back. Not even a portion of it any longer."

"I'm not sure what this entails with doing this your way, but I'm willing to listen. This business was my grandfather's, and he loved it here. And the people that worked here." He glanced over at his father as he continued to argue with Ethan about loyalty. "Dad has been falling down on the job in other areas of his life as well. We came in today thinking that this was a meeting about helping us out of a little trouble. I had no idea it was this bad. As you said, he's been lying to us for some time now. Do you think you can help us out a little? Break it to him that he has to go?"

"Yes, it would be my pleasure. As for the rest of it, I would say that's about right." She looked at Mr. Allen when he finally shut up. "You're fired."

~~~

Elliot was still laughing about what his dad had told him. She had just turned to the man who had been in charge of the company for nearly four decades and fired him. Then, when he started blustering around about how she couldn't do that, Hannah had called in security, and with the permission of his sons, had the man tossed out on his ass. He wished now that he could have been with her instead of working on this project here. This one wasn't nearly as entertaining.

His family had been a part of the trials of the Vampire League since before he'd been born. And once a month one of them would come here and help pass judgment on the vampires that had broken a law. Enough of a law that they would need to be brought before the council. It was pretty boring, and that was why they each took a turn in sitting where he was right now.

Those boys of his, they'll make this work, I'm thinking. Hannah told me that they had some skeletons in their closets too, but nothing like their daddy had. He told his dad that he was glad it had worked out. *You know it. I would have hated to have closed that place down. We helped them build it, didn't we? Back in the day.*

I think you might be right on that. But that's true for a lot of the buildings around here, don't you think? I think we even helped out with the jail and courthouse. His dad laughed, and Elliot asked him where they were headed now.

She's been really busy, that wife of yours. I gave her a list of companies that we have a vested interest in, and she got right on them. Right now we're headed over to the courthouse to get some land information on the Melvin business. She seems to think that they are encroaching on the land next to them and taking away some of their land. I didn't know this was a problem, but she told me that if they were taking the land and not paying the proper taxes on it, someone could go to jail. This girl knows her business.

She does at that. He realized that he hadn't been paying attention very well, and started taking notes on things he heard. *Dad just make sure that she's careful. I don't want her hurt.*

You can count on me, son. We're about to go and have some lunch, then we're hitting the last two of the businesses that need a pep talk. Not that she's all that peppy when she tells them like it is, but I'm having the time of my life. His dad was still laughing as he closed the connection.

"Mr. Crosby, are you paying attention?" He told Donald Shalwar that he was. Elliot, even his whole family, hated this prick. "Then tell me, what would be your opinion on this man's case. If you were paying attention, I'm sure that we don't have to repeat it."

As a matter of course, he did know what was going on with this man. So had Hannah when she helped him with the list of people they were going to see today. Pulling out his notes, Donald snickered. Elliot wanted to knock the man's head off.

"Mr. Cohibin has been going through some rough times of it. He's lost his job recently, as well as his mate was killed. To say that he'd stolen for no reason is a falsehood. He was trying to provide for his family as best he could." Elliot pulled out the next sheet of paper, listing the number of times that he'd gone to the council to ask for help. "You've all spoken to him over the last few months. He's come here on numerous occasions to not only ask for assistance, but to beg that he could bring his family here, to be safe while he looked for work long term."

"Where are you getting this information? It's not right, wherever you got it." He looked at where she had put notes on the dates and times that she'd gotten information from the log here. "We'll hear no more about this. We're here to pass judgment on his stealing from one of his own."

"Everyone is required to sign in when they arrive and when they leave, correct? This information is then downloaded onto a program that I told you wasn't secure. I just took advantage of your laziness to get to it to use." Donald, one of the oldest men on the board with the exception of him, waved him off. "It states right here that you, on two different occasions, had him tossed to the street rather than listen to anything he had to say. I also know that the man that he supposedly stole from is your own son. Could it be that you and he are lying, and not this man?"

"I will point out yet again to you, Elliot, that this is no place for you to place blame on others." He asked him if he wasn't doing the same to Mr. Cohibin. "No, he was caught stealing from my son, and that's what we're here to talk about. Not whether or not it's true."

Elliot only looked around at the other board members, and he could see the concern written on their faces as well. He was sure that they were thinking that was just what they were here for. But he could see that a couple of them were also going to say something. Before that, he had his last bit of information that he wanted to unload, thanks to his lovely mate.

"I have information in regard to the theft in question. I've been told that the things that were stolen from your son didn't belong to him in the first place. That they belonged to another member of this realm. He was told that if he didn't want to go along with what was being told to him, that you, Donald, would have him brought up on charges that would make those against this innocent man seem like child's play." Donald stood up, and was told to sit down by another council member. "I have it right here, should you want to see it. There are documents that state that Donald and his son have been harassing the other gentleman, until he had no choice but to leave here."

Even as he was being dragged out of the room, Donald was screaming that he was innocent. His only crime had been caring for his own children in this. The child that he was referring to was nearly three hundred years old, Elliot thought, and well ready to be taking care of his own needs. Mr. Cohibin was told he could go, and was compensated nicely by the council in the form of money as well as a good job. They should have done this months ago.

Elliot was gathering up his things after the last judgement was passed. Richard, another member of the board, asked him if he could speak to him for a moment.

"Where did you get this information, Elliot? I, for one, would like to meet this other person that does such grand work." He told him it was his mate. "Ah, the baby vampire. I've heard great things about her. She is going to go far in her line of work, I think."

"She's working with our firm now. Helping my dad out this afternoon, as a matter of fact." He had always respected Richard. He was a good man with a hard task set before him. Richard asked him if she might be willing to help them out with a few matters. "I don't think she'll have a problem with that. However, you'd have to ask her. I'm her mate, but I don't tell her what to do."

Richard laughed, and then sat back in the chair he'd been sitting in. There was more to this than him just wanting to talk to her about some cases he had. When he asked him to have a seat, Elliot did so, but he didn't want to. There was no way that what Richard was going to say could be good.

"The spot that Donald has vacated is open, and I'd like for you to take it." Whatever Elliot had thought he was going to say, that wasn't it. Elliot tried to think what this would mean to him and Hannah. "There are perks to being here with the council. And I'm going to tell you right now, you do not have to live around here. So long as you're available when we need you, then I for one have no problem where you reside."

"I'd have to talk to Hannah and my family." He said that he would expect no less from him. "This isn't what I thought you were going to tell me. I thought you were going to say something along the lines of telling you when I have that sort of damaging information."

"No, you did good work on this, both you and Hannah. There might have been a different outcome should you have not come through for him. As it is now, we have a good man working for us who will be able to keep his children close to him. And someone off the board that was as toxic as anything else that might harm us." He nodded, thinking that Donald should have been taken off it long ago. "You will talk to her about this? If you need someone to come and convince her, I can do that too."

"You've never met my Hannah, or you'd know that no one changes her mind if she's set on something. She's smart and open-minded—I know that doesn't seem like it—but she follows her own heart, not what someone might say about her decision on something." Richard nodded but didn't move on yet. "What else is going on?"

"You've come a long way in coming here and passing judgment on people. And I have to tell you that I do look forward to coming in when I know that you'll be the one here with me. But today you took it out of the ball park, as humans are so fond of saying. I'm impressed." He told him it was his mate. "Maybe she gathered the information for you, but you're the one that brought it here and did such a beautiful job of getting it done. For some, just having the right thing to say or do doesn't make them smart at what they're saying."

Elliot knew that as well. And when Richard told him he'd

be in touch, he figured that he was going to be calling him a lot to get him to come work for the council. Elliot wasn't sure how he felt about it. Good and bad, he supposed. But one thing was certain, he wasn't going to make any move without talking to Hannah first.

He got home just after three in the afternoon. He would have thought that Hannah and his dad would have been home by now. Wandering through the house, a scent had him turning back to the front hall where he'd entered the house. There had been a stranger in the house, and he might well be here still.

Elliot didn't want to alarm his family, and certainly not Hannah. As he made his way around the bottom floor, all he could think about was Cody and where he was. Going up the stairs two at a time, he was just on the landing when Duncan came out of Cody's bedroom. He had a gun to the little guy's head.

"We're walking out of here, and you're going to keep yourself away from us. He's my boy to do what I want to him." Elliot asked Cody if he was all right. "What do you care if he's all right or not? He's my kid and I'll tell him how he's feeling, and I'm taking him home with me."

Elliot wasn't going to let him go anywhere. Especially not with his son. He looked right at Cody and told him that it would be fine, to not fight him. Duncan started talking about his house needing cleaning and how the kid wasn't around for him to beat up. When he heard a sound behind him, Elliot didn't even bother turning. He'd know the sound of those footsteps anywhere.

Chapter 12

Hannah had had enough of people to last her several lifetimes. But spending the day with such an old-world charmer had made her smile more often than she was angry. People were dicks for the most part, and she was glad every day that she had a place that she could go to and get away from them.

She and Franklin were having dinner when he suddenly stood up. She did as well. They'd been brought their check, and she worried that there was something wrong about it.

"He's in trouble." She asked him who, as she was gathering her coat and purse. "Elliot. Not trouble, but he's a little tense. I can feel it. And for him to be tense about anything, it's got to be bad."

"You're not helping me." He took her hand as they exited the restaurant, and before she could comment, if she had anything to say, they were standing in front of her home. She looked at Franklin. "I'm afraid."

"Don't be. I've not spoken to him as yet, but as I said, he's tense, but not angry or upset that much." She kissed him on the cheek. "Now that was very nice of you. Come now, we'll have a looksee on what's going on, and try not to get in Elliot's way when he tells us to."

Nodding, she went to the door and opened it quietly. When she closed it behind them, Hannah glanced around and saw Elliot standing at the top of the stairs. For all accounts he looked like he was all right, but then she heard the second voice and her anger surged up high.

"You just get your ass out of my way and I won't have to hurt you none. I'm leaving here with shit for brains, and there isn't a damned thing you can do about it." She made her way up the stairs and stood beside Elliot. He kissed her on the cheek before explaining to her what was going on.

"So you see, not only has he broken into our home, but he's also admitted to trying to kidnap our son. I'm really pissed off that he got into my home in the first place, and I'd like nothing more than to rip his head off and be done with him." She didn't even ask Elliot if he could actually do that, and looked at the man and boy as he continued. "I've contacted the police. They should be here momentarily. Joey asked me not to kill him until he's here. But if I had to, then so be it."

"I'm fucking standing right here. What do you mean, you're going to take my head off?" Duncan laughed. "You moron, I'm the one with the hostage and the gun here. You're not doing shit to me."

"Elliot, please don't kill him. We've only just had the carpet cleaned, and I'm sure that they'll be very upset with us if you get blood on it again." Cody laughed, and she got down on her knees to look at him. "You're going to be just fine. And when this nonsense is over, we're going to go out to dinner and celebrate. All right?"

"Yes. I'd like that. But no more burgers, please. They're good and all, but I've had enough for a while." She wondered when he'd tell her that. He'd been asking for burgers every meal for two weeks. "Maybe we can go get spaghetti. I like the garlic bread that they—"

The gun came down hard on Cody's head, and it was all she could do not to leap at Duncan and tear him apart on her own. But she stood up and put her hands on her hips before confronting the idiot.

"I've had just about enough of you and your shit. You are to put that fucking gun away, or so help me, I'm going to come over there and get it and shoot you myself." Duncan just laughed at her. "All right then, how about if I send my husband after you? You won't think it's so funny when he's finished with you."

"He's a pussy. Letting you run things around here. Why, before you came here, he was begging me to let his little boy go." She didn't even bother looking at Elliot, she knew better. And so did he. "Get out of my way and we'll be out of your hair."

"You're not going anywhere with him. I told you that several times now."

For a moment Hannah was afraid that Elliot was going to attack, but about that time, Joey from the police department said he was coming up.

"Mr. Wayne, I've got a warrant for your arrest. I can add kidnapping to it too, but I don't think you'll live long enough for me to get it written up. Let the boy go and you might make it to trial." Duncan asked if he was going to kill him. "No, not me. But Elliot here will. Or any of the other members of his family. They're all here too—every Crosby is downstairs waiting to see who gets to kill you."

"You're going to just let them murder me? I'm a good citizen." He asked him if he had killed Tim James and Rose Wayne. "I don't know that first name, but my wife ran off. I don't know whose body you found under my porch. Perhaps this man here put it there to frame me so he could take my son."

She watched her brother carefully. He was insane, she could see that now. Not only did he think that it was his right as his parent to beat the boy, he'd made him watch as he'd killed his own mother. That alone should put him in prison for the rest of his days, but then she didn't run the court systems. What she was actually afraid of was that he'd plead insanity and be out in a few years. That wouldn't be helpful to anyone, especially Cody.

I'm going to have to kill him. You know as well as I do that he'll get out soon. She told Elliot that was what she was thinking, that he was insane. *Then you agree that I should take him out of our lives for good?*

No, I didn't say that. What I said was, I agree with you in that he'll be around bothering us a lot longer. But I have a plan. He growled and she looked up at him. *I have a plan, and that's going to save me from having to visit you in prison. Now behave until I can't get him to stop this nonsense.*

I'll agree, but the moment that he hurts you, all bets are off and I'm going to beat your ass for getting hurt. She smiled at him. *Don't give me that look. You know that I can do it.*

I know you can, but you're very kind in letting me try and do it my way. He grumbled again but she stood up. *Just don't attack him until I tell you to. I don't want Cody hurt in all this.*

Walking toward Duncan and Cody, she smiled. Hannah wondered if they could tell it wasn't a happy smile, but so long as he was watching her and not hitting Cody, she didn't care. As soon as she was close enough to touch them both, she drew back her fist and slammed it right into her brother's face.

When he fell back on his ass, she told Cody to go to Elliot. Hannah stepped her foot on Duncan's throat to hold him down. This shit was going to hell in a handbasket, as her Grammy used to say. Picking up the gun that he'd dropped, she held it in the same position that Duncan had, but pointed at his head this time.

"You're a fucking moron, did you know that?" She realized that he couldn't speak, but that wasn't her problem. "Why didn't you just kill yourself off and leave your family alone? I'm sure that they would have gotten along a lot better without you around. Now, I'm going to lift my foot up enough for you to speak. If you don't say something stupid, I won't snap your neck like a twig. Understand me?"

He nodded, and she lifted her foot up enough that he could breathe and talk, but he had to know that she'd bring it down hard if he fucked up. When he took in big gulping breaths of air, she put the gun on his forehead. She did not trust him.

"You think you're all brave and shit because you have a gun, don't you?" She asked him if that was how him having a gun made him feel. "I'm a brave man anyway. I came here to get my boy, and here you go trying to hurt me. You're the one that kidnapped him from me. And I'm going to tell everybody that'll listen that's what you did."

177

"Good luck with that. The Crosbys are a highly respected family, and you're the man that murdered his wife while your son watched. Then you had him help you take her and put her under the porch. Is that about right? Or did I miss something?" He spoke again. "Oh yeah, the little boy under there. Thanks for reminding me. Yes, you did kill him. They have found enough evidence on his body to not just convict you, but to also let you rot in your cell when they're done with you."

"They can't do that to me, can they?" Hannah just shrugged. "Not that it matters. I'm going to get off from all of this shit. They can't arrest me for the same crime two times. They fucked up, and now I'm a free man."

"So, you did kill your wife." He nodded. "I'm sorry, I can't hear you. Did you or did you not kill your own wife and make your son watch?"

"He's just lucky that I didn't smother him too. The fucking little shit. Had I known that he was going to be this much trouble, I would have knocked him out of her the first chance I got. He's been nothing but a pain in my ass since." She asked him again if he had killed Rose and made Cody watch. "Hell yeah, I killed her. She was doing shit that would piss me off. Having a good time in the kitchen with that brat. She's just lucky that I didn't kill her sooner."

She didn't even bother looking at Joey. The camera had been on the two of them since she'd joined Duncan. The things he was saying now would go a long way in keeping him behind bars where he belonged. Forever.

"What do you think is going to happen to me, bitch? I'll tell you, nothing. I'm a free man because they didn't take the time to read me my rights." She said that they had. "Sure, they did it. They're both dead, aren't they? And no one is going to be able to arrest me for it. And as for getting out, I didn't have to do any more than say that they'd not read me my rights, and I got a get out of jail free card from them. Imagine my surprise when it worked."

"Yes, well, I can imagine a lot of things at the moment involving you. None of which is going to make you very happy, I'm afraid." She lifted the gun from his forehead and looked down at Duncan. "You had a good wife and a little boy. Money in the bank that you never told Rose about, as well as freedom to do whatever you wanted. And what did you do? You killed someone, and then didn't have the balls to admit what you'd done and have her buried in a nice cemetery. You're a cold and heartless son of a bitch—you know that, don't you?"

"You're just jealous." Hannah asked him how he'd come up with that. "You're jealous of me because I can do whatever I want and get away with it. And as soon as they let me out of the cell, because they have nothing to hold me on, then I'm going to get my boy and he's going to regret pissing me off by running away."

"You go on thinking that, all the way to death row. And you should also know that Rose was planning to leave you. She had the means and the way to get away. Someone came forward when she didn't show up where they were supposed to meet. He has a different story than the one you're telling." He asked her what this other person was saying. "Rose? She was a good deal smarter than you think. We have you on video killing that young boy. And how you did it. Also, and this is the most sickening thing I've ever heard of, we have you murdering your wife. Each and every sick minute of it."

"You lie. She didn't have the smarts to do that. Not unless you told her to. That's it, isn't it? You came to my house and put in cameras so that you could catch me at something." He laughed. "I'm afraid that won't work either. I didn't give you permission to enter my house and hang them up."

"She lived there and paid the bills with money that she earned taking in sewing. What you didn't take from her, that is. So she didn't need permission to do things to the house. When you married her, you gave her that right. And I think she was pretty damned smart for taking precautions." He looked around now, worry seeming to mar his forehead. "What's wrong, Duncan? Are you afraid that I'm telling you the truth?"

Duncan was helped up when she stepped back. Joey stood by her, and when he asked, she handed him the gun. He didn't say anything for several moments, but she could almost hear his questions. So, when he asked, she had answers for him.

"Did she put in cameras?" She nodded and gave him the paperwork that Rose had left in her bedside drawer from when she'd paid for it. "And the rest, it's true too? Not that I doubt you—I've heard that you're a stickler for facts—but did she plan to leave him?"

"Yes. However, the man who was helping her, he needs to not be bothered. He helps a lot of women out that are trying to leave their husbands. It's a sort of underground network for getting abused people out of bad places." He said that he could do that. "I think Rose had figured out that she'd never make it out alive. But for Cody, she made sure that he was in good hands. He told me that she had him go to the greenhouse because there wasn't anyone better at keeping him safe than the Crosbys."

"I agree. Thank you for your help. I don't think we would have gotten a confession out of him without your help."

When Joey left her to take Duncan away, she went to Elliot. In his arms was just where she wanted to be.

~~~

Elliot waited on someone to say something. They were all sitting around the family table looking like they were thinking hard. He didn't think it was all that difficult of a question. Did they think that he should take the job or not? Once Hannah had told him she thought he'd be good at it, to take the job, he went to run it by his family.

"This job, what is it you're going to be doing? I understand that you'll be sort of the jury for crimes that vampires commit, but that can't be an everyday thing, can it?" Elliot told Jason that they did it once a week, and they put the ones from the previous week into the work load. "Yeah, I guess I knew that. When it was my turn, I remember it being about a dozen of them throughout the week. But the rest of the time, what will you be doing? I'd be bored out of my mind if I had a job that only had you working one day a week."

"There is going to be much more research done on cases than before. Not just for our needs, but for the people that are coming before us for one reason or another." Elliot looked at Hannah as he continued. "We're going to take the job together, and make sure that there is some justice for everyone."

"Well, I must say that I'm very proud of you, son. You've come a long way if you were to ask me. A mate and a good job. Not that you need it, but it does help when you have something to look forward to." He thanked his dad. "And I like the idea that you don't have to think it's your doom as soon as you're

181

called in to the council. I remember once, long ago, that they called me in. For three days I could neither sleep nor feed. It was like I was going to the gallows, and there hadn't been a trial yet."

"What did they need from you, Dad?" Elliot wanted to know as well, and when his brother Sean asked, he smiled. "You didn't get into trouble, did you?"

"Oh no, not me. They wanted me to come in and tell them about our ability to be out in the sun. Of course I didn't tell them the entire story, not about who we saved that night, only that someone very powerful had given it to us when we all helped." Sean asked if they believed him. "I was never sure about that. I do know that they had a man or two follow us around for a time, I guess trying to figure out what we really were doing. But like a lot of things with this council board, they got bored and stopped looking."

Elliot could vaguely remember that. His dad having them dart in and out of businesses, sometimes pulling shadows around them when there didn't seem to be anyone around. He'd made it into a game. They were really too old for such things, but like most people that had been around for too long, they would do just about anything to stave off the feeling of being useless, or for that matter, bored.

They all agreed that they'd be perfect for the job. Even Hannah, who hadn't thought about how much she could help, was agreeable to what the council wanted from them. She even suggested that they put the money that they paid them aside, to use to help families of the men that were found guilty of their crimes. He told his family about that, and they were all in agreement that they'd help too. It was a good cause.

They were walking home after that. The nights were still chilly, but it was warming up again. As they walked hand in hand, Elliot thought of how lucky he'd been, and that he had all that a man could ask for. More than any vampire had deserved.

"Cody's paperwork came through this morning. The judge has expedited things for us so that he can have a different name when his father goes to trial." Hannah told him that was wonderful news. "Also, I've ordered a pretty headstone for his mom. I didn't put anything on it about Duncan, but I did say that she was a beloved mother and a good friend. I showed him pictures of it just before we left. I think I made him sad."

"He's all right. I think he's just glad to have this all done. He told me that he was glad that he didn't have to be watching out for his dad all the time. And he did sleep better last night. I think he needed closure on all of this." Elliot said that he agreed, and looked in the window of the jewelry store, his planned destination. He asked Hannah if she wanted to go in.

"Sure, but don't buy me anything. I have a car and more things than I've had in a long time. You don't have to buy me something every time we go out." Elliot just kissed her on the mouth as he opened the door. "You are not as charming as you think you are."

He just smiled as he led her to the wedding rings. He had hoped that she'd pick out the one that he'd had engraved for her, but watched her face instead of what she might be looking at. When she started to step away, he asked her which one she'd try on if he promised her he wouldn't buy it for her after this. She agreed, but didn't ask for a ring right away.

"I would like to try on that sapphire one. The way it sparkles in the light makes me think of the faeries in our back yard." The ring was the one he'd already paid for. Elliot was so thrilled he almost forgot to ask her to marry him, to make it legal when he was handed the ring. "What are you doing? Get up from there. Elliot, you said that you'd not buy this for me."

"I already did. See? The inscription has our names in it." She took the ring from him and looked at it. "It says that E. C. is in love with H.C., just as I wanted it to say."

He pulled her hand to his mouth and kissed the back of it. Then he put the ring on her wedding finger and looked up at her. Christ, he thought, there couldn't be a man more in love with someone than he was at this very moment.

"Hannah, will you consent to being my wife? The mother of my children, whether from your body or just our hearts? Will you love me for as long as I love you? And keep me in line when I need it?" She told him that the last thing might be too hard for her. "I have all the faith in you in the world. Will you be my wife?"

"Yes. I will be your wife, Elliot Crosby." The room erupted in clapping and laughter. His family was there, as was the minister, who was going to marry them today. Even her sister Julia and her brood of children. "What is all this?"

"You said yes, and I'm not taking any chances that you'll back out. I want to do this now. Cody has agreed to be my best man in this, so we're ready." She pressed her body to his, kissing him in the process. "What was that for? Not that I'm complaining, but that was supposed to happen after he says we're man and wife."

"Because I love you with all my heart, and then some. And spending the rest of my life with you will be the greatest pleasure of all time."

Elliot kissed her back and held her in his arms as the quick ceremony was completed. In less time than it had taken for him to pick out her ring, he was married to the woman of his dreams, and he could not be happier.

They all met back at their home. No gifts were brought to them, which he was quite happy about. They had been around for a very long time, him and his family, and they had very little use for anything more. And what they did need, they could simply buy it. All the money that would have been spent on gifts, he asked for them to donate to the charity of their choice.

The wedding dinner was a bit more crowded than the wedding had been. His dad had been in charge of inviting people, and he wished now that he'd asked him to take it easy. There had to be over two hundred people roaming around their home, and most of them he didn't have a clue who they were. It wasn't until Emerald and Jewel stood beside him that he felt better.

"Who the fuck are all these people? If you want, I can get them out of here for you." She winked at him when he thanked her but said he'd take care of it. "Well, if you change your mind, I'm armed with not just my dragons, but swords too." With that, she simply walked away.

"She's not really good around strangers." Elliot told Jewel she wasn't all that good around people she knew either. "Yes, I guess you're right. But she has been good to me. And this wedding is beautiful. Even Emerald said so."

"Do you know any of these people? I'm assuming that some of them are from the town, but I haven't any idea who would be who." She laughed when he did. Her laughter was like a balm to an open wound. Soft and healing.

185

"Some of them are from the town, but not all. There is the pack master there, and he had a few guests with him. Mostly his own children, but they have a few others that wanted to come too. I believe that is the mayor over there. I don't have much use for the pompous windbag, but I didn't vote so I can't complain too much." Elliot asked her if she would have voted for him, given the chance. "No. I've only just been made aware of a few things, and I'm having Hannah help me out so I can see if they're true or not. I think they are, but until then, I'm going to hold my tongue and say nothing. For now. When I get the information that I think I will, then I'm going to have him murdered."

When she too walked away, Elliot shook his head. These women were his family, but he'd been surprised at how violent they'd all become. He wondered if it had anything to do with Emerald, and shook his head. Of course it did. She was a dragon warrior, and she could and would hurt you if you didn't listen to her. Elliot decided to go and find his lovely bride, and see if he could get her in the closet for a quick and satisfying love making session.

Chapter 13

How often did a person get arrested for something that they didn't do? Alex had been wondering that for the last few days. While he sat in a jail cell waiting on his dad to come and get him, he had a lot of time to think. Or for his dad to help him find out why they thought that he'd killed a woman and help him get out of jail. He looked over at the man who touched his arm.

Alex was deaf. He could read lips really well, but only if you were facing him. But he couldn't make sounds that made the words he was trying to say very clearly. As he'd been born this way, he had no idea what words sounded like. Nor what he did when he said them.

He watched the man's mouth as it moved. "You are being called from out in the hall. I'm not sure how many times they said it, but I'd go over there." He nodded and made his way to the bars that held him and several other men in the same cell.

He couldn't read the man's mouth that was speaking. He

looked at the man next to him, Roman, he thought he'd said his name was, and he told him that his dad was there, and that he wanted to talk to him. Thanking Roman, he nodded at the officer.

Taken down the long hall that he'd been brought down three days ago, he kept his head up so in case someone wanted to speak to him, he could see it. The officers, for the most part, were all right, but there were a couple that he would just as soon avoid if he could.

When he was seated in the chair with his chains around his arms shackled to the table, he nearly cried when his dad came in the room. They couldn't touch, but he felt his dad's love for him as powerfully as if he had hugged him. Dad sat down across from him and asked him if he was all right.

It was difficult to sign with his wrists so tightly bound to the table. But his dad seemed to understand what he was saying. When his dad said that he was looking into things, Alex felt the relief of it all the way to his feet.

"I've called your sister. She's none too happy about things right now, as you can well imagine. She's got a burr up her butt about something out where she is, and said she'd come here as soon as she could get a flight out." He asked him what she was upset about. "Some person she works with would like to see much more of her, but she's not having it. I guess it got a little out of hand and she hurt him."

Alex laughed when his dad did. His sister was a hellion and could beat the best of men when she was pissed off. Misty was a loving, friendly person, but she could turn on you so fast and severely that you'd never know what hit you. He loved her very much.

His dad told him what he'd been able to find out. Yes, there had been an accident, and yes, a woman had been killed. What his dad didn't understand was why they thought that Alex had done it. He would like to know that too. Alex didn't even know how to drive, much less run over someone while doing it.

"I'm having my attorney look into a few things. He's got some hotshot person who does research for this sort of thing. But I don't know about this guy he has looking. He seems to be doing a half-baked job of it so far as I can tell. I guess his best has gone on her own and is running a nice firm in Ohio. I'm going to contact her tonight. I want the best working on this for you, Alex, never doubt that."

He didn't, and told his dad that. But he was worried. This was murder, and he was in a town that he didn't know well nor was he well known. His dad told him that he'd be back in the morning, and if he thought of something to let him know in the morning. Alex was taken back to his cell. This time there was no one in it with him.

Alex was used to his own company. Even in a room full of people he felt like he was alone. He knew it was because others had no idea how to relate to him. They didn't think, he supposed, that he was normal, and they treated him as such. But Misty didn't. She was hell bent on leather, a statement he'd never understood, on making everyone dislike her. Laughing, he thought of the last time he'd spoken to her.

"I've about had it with men." He nodded, knowing that she'd be the first person in the world to admit to that and really mean it. "Why are they so pigheaded and such assholes?"

"I don't know. I'm not like that, am I?" She hugged him and told him that he'd never be like the majority or she'd kick his ass. "So loving. No wonder men hate you back."

Of course she had taken it as a compliment and not as an insult as he'd meant for it to be. They talked for a long time often, him on his special computer-based telephone and her on her cell. Sometimes the words would come up wrong, but he understood her. She was the only woman in the world that he'd ever love. He knew that, and she teased him about it all the time.

"Someday you're going to find you a woman that will whip you into shape and make you the toast of the town." He asked her what that meant. "I don't know. This guy today said it to me. I just smiled and went about my business. Do you suppose there is anyone out there, for either of us?"

"I don't know. I'd like to think there is, but I just don't know." He waited for her to reply, and he wasn't surprised when she told him that there was someone out there for him. Just not her. She was too caustic and mean. "I love you more than anything in this world, and don't you think I'd tell you if you were being too caustic and mean?"

"No, you'd tell me to behave and shut my trap. You have before, you know." He laughed and she sent him happy faces. "When I come home again, we'll go out and have some fun. You living with dad, it must put a damper on your sex life."

"My sex life is just fine, thank you very much." He knew that she'd not think so, but that didn't matter to him. Women liked him because he was different, but no one would love him because he was different. He didn't like thinking like that. It made him sound whiney. "I'd very much like to take you out to dinner when you get home. I've been doing research for restaurants around the state, and it's been fun for Dad and me.

He drives, and we get, for the most part, a good meal out of it."

She was proud of him too. He knew that she'd kick his ass if he let himself go, just sitting around not working or doing anything productive. Because of her and her bullying him for most of his life, he had a job and some friends. But most importantly, he wasn't as socially backward as most deaf people he knew. Misty would never let him feel sorry for himself.

He felt the vibration of the cell being opened and opened his eyes. He watched the two men as they entered the cell with him. They were different than the others had been. These men were well dressed. When they approached the bed he was lying on, he felt his body tense up for the pain.

The first guy hit him as he was leaping from the bed. The second man, trying his best to grab hold of him, was knocked out when Alex threw him against the concrete wall. The first man had a gun, and when he pointed it at him, Alex lunged forward, knocking the man back and hitting his head on the bed frame. He was waiting for either man to get up when he was grabbed from behind. It took his terrified mind a few minutes to realize that it was someone trying to help him.

"Are you all right?" He nodded and pointed to the two men. "I don't know who they are, but they sure meant you some harm. I'm going to call this in, but you must wait over there. If this goes south, I want you to run, all right? Then call your dad. He'll come for you, right?"

He didn't know how to tell this man that he couldn't call his dad, but he'd try. There wasn't a lot of pay phones around, and none of them had any way for him type in his message to his dad.

The officer seemed to understand his limitations and

handed him his cell phone. He could text his dad with this and he'd come for him. Standing against the wall, he watched the man as he checked pulses on the two men and then took the gun away. As they were being cuffed, two other officers came down the hall.

Something was off about them. Alex slowly made his way to the bars where the door was as the two men pulled out their guns. He knew that they were going to hurt him — Alex didn't know why he thought that, but he was still shocked when they fired their weapons at the two men that were down. Then they shot the cop.

Moving out the door while they checked on weapons and such, he was down the hallway to the big door just as it opened again. Alex stood behind it and grabbed the door before it swung back closed. Whatever was going on in here, he wasn't going to be a part of it.

Getting out of the station was easier than he'd thought it would be. He was calm on the outside, but a mess in his mind. Walking slowly out of the building, he grabbed a jacket that was lying on the bench and kept moving.

Standing on the sidewalk, he tried to get his bearings. There wasn't any place that he could go that he knew would be safe. Rounding the corner of the building, he found himself in an alley that was open at the other end. Moving to the other side of the dumpster, he pulled out the phone and messaged his dad.

Come get me. I'm in deep trouble. When his dad didn't answer right away, he remembered that this wasn't his phone. *Dad, it's Alex. Someone tried to kill me in the cell. I got out but now I'm afraid.*

Where are you, son? He told him and waited on him to reply. *Don't leave there until I tell you do. There is a shit storm going on, and I'm worried for you.*

He told him he was worried too. When the police started to fan out of the building, Alex moved deeper into the alley. The opening at the other end was clear, but he wasn't going to go anywhere until he heard from his dad. Thinking of Misty, he messaged her, remembering to let her know it was him and telling her what dad had said.

Alex, Dad is with me – run. He felt his heart sort of freeze up and read the next message from her. *He didn't get a message from you. Find a building. Hide. But get rid of that phone. Destroy it.*

Breaking the phone in half, he also took out the sim card with the battery. Dumping the phone in the dumpster, he made his way to the opposite end of the alley just as three cops came around the corner. They were checking out the dumpster when he entered the building next to the station.

Alex walked for six blocks, keeping an eye out for any police or anyone that looked suspicious. Everyone did, so that didn't help, but he finally found a place that he could hide in and found himself a dark corner. He tried to slow his heart and mind down while he tried to think.

Those men had tried to kill him. And would have had he not felt the vibration on the bars. Being aware, Misty always told him, would someday save his life. And she'd been correct. They could have come into the cell without him knowing, shot him to hell and back, and no one would be the wiser.

He had to get in touch with his dad and sister. But to do that, he would need either a cell phone or a computer, neither of which were where he was. He'd have to find something else soon or they would catch him. And this time it would be for the murder of a cop, of that he had no doubt.

Thinking about his dad, he wondered how they had gotten the phone hacked so that he thought he was talking to him. Had he not messaged Misty, again, he would have been walking right into a trap.

Moving around a little to get comfortable, he kept a close watch on everything around him. He knew on some level that he couldn't see or smell anything more than a person of hearing, but he liked to think that he could. It gave him a feeling of having the upper hand when he knew that he did not.

He must have dozed off at some point, because when he woke he was sore and disorientated. Looking around, careful of where he stepped on the broken glass all round him, he looked out the window and tried to figure out where he could go to be safe. Here he knew he was exposed to everyone and anything that came in the building. He couldn't hear, nor would he be able to shout out for help.

As he stood there, something touched his shoulder and he turned and punched out at the same time. When the man fell back, he didn't move, but did stare up at him from his position on the floor. He held out a cell phone, which he did not take.

"I'm a friend of your sisters, Misty." He didn't move. "My name is Sean Crosby. If you'd message her, she'll tell you that I've come to get you to take you to my home. She'll meet us there. And I'm supposed to tell you that her birthday was last week, and you didn't give her a card. She seemed most upset about that too."

He hadn't sent her a card. Alex had forgotten that the post didn't run on Sunday, and by then it was too late anyway. Taking the phone from the man, he messaged Misty and told her what was going on. The picture that came up on the camera

194

was the man on the floor still.

Go with him. He's a vampire friend of mine, and he'll take you to his home. He's a good man, Alex. Dad and I will meet you there in two days. We're taking our time to get to you. Alex messaged her back that he didn't trust this man. *Most people you shouldn't trust, honey, but I promise you, he's one of the good guys. I'd bet my life on it.*

"Are you ready to go?" The man knew sign language and sat up so that he could answer him if need be. "I'm going to take you by way of a vampire. It can be a little dizzying at first, so keep your eyes closed while we travel. All right?"

Almost as soon as he nodded, the man was wrapped behind him and they moved. Alex held on tightly, sure that he was going to be dropped or something. But when he looked around when they stopped, he could see that he was in a nice bedroom. Alex was so grateful that he cried. He'd never been so afraid in his life.

~~~

Misty hated men. Okay, she thought. That wasn't really a fair statement, not even for her. She hated ninety-nine-point nine percent of them, and she'd yet to find the point one percent that she might like. Men were, for the most part, jackasses. And while she supposed there were a few nice guys out there, her dad and brother to name a couple, she didn't like having to deal with them. She could never have a conversation with one without them looking at her chest. She had, on more than one occasion, jerked their head up to look at her, not her attributes. Except for one man.

Sean Crosby had been in college when she had been. He wasn't anyone that she would have taken notice of. A great looking guy, sure, but those type of men were annoying, and she avoided them as much as possible. Then one night he had come to her rescue and saved her life.

She knew better than to walk home after dark. But her stupid car hadn't started, again, and she didn't want to sleep in her car. Misty had thought that might be just as dangerous. Boy oh boy, had she been wrong.

The men had come out of nowhere. She'd thought that she was being followed, but whenever she looked around all she could see was more darkness. It wasn't until the man in front of her hit her with something hard that she knew she was going to die. Falling back, she was caught and fought the man holding her. It was Sean.

"Are you all right?" Nodding hurt her head, and he grinned at her. "I'm sorry you're going to find out about me this way, but I don't have a choice now. Just don't move." She didn't have any idea what he was talking about until she sat up enough to watch what was going on before her.

The men—four of them—were taunting Sean. He was in the middle of them as they circled around him. Misty wanted to get up and help him, but she knew that she'd just be in the way. And then he moved.

Had she not been looking when she did, she was sure that she would have missed it. He killed the first man quickly. When he dropped to the ground, she could see from her vantage point on the ground that his neck had been broken.

The second man didn't fare any better, but he was killed when Sean's hand seemed to just morph into a long blade and cut his throat. Even then, the man seemed to just flop all over the place, like he was trying his best to not be dying. Sickened by the movement slowing, she looked at the last two men.

"You aren't taking our prize." The third man was talking to Sean, who just laughed. "We weren't going to kill her, and now look what you've done. Killed our friends. We're going to have to hurt you bad for that."

She had thought then and now that the man had to have a couple of screws loose. Did he not see that Sean had halved his manpower? In just a matter of seconds? She thought that was the first time in her life that she realized that men were stupid. Most anyway. But Sean had killed the other man in seconds, then pulled the fourth one to his mouth and bit down on him.

She wasn't faint of heart, nor was she someone that was squeamish about things. But to watch him drinking from the man made her think that he was going to kill her next. And that thought had her moving back from him when he dropped the last man to the ground.

"I'd never harm you, Misty. On this you have my word." She wanted to believe him, but there was a spot of blood on his lip and she couldn't stop staring at it. "Come on then. Let's get you home."

Even with her things surrounding her, she still felt...dirty was the name for it. She wanted to take a shower and scrub all night, but she was afraid to be alone. Sean seemed to understand that and sat down on the couch and turned on the television. Then he told her to take a warm shower and he'd be right there.

After that, even when she knew that he could be doing anything but hanging out with her, they were together. There was nothing sexual about their friendship, but it was a tight bond. Then one night he told her all about himself. That he was a very old and very powerful vampire.

"Why did you help me? You could have just, I don't know, killed them, then me too. Why did you save me?" He laughed, and she smacked him on the arm. "I'm serious. Why me of all people?"

"You make me laugh. And even though you avoided me a great deal, I could tell that you were a nice person and I wanted to get to know you. I knew when I first met you that I could trust you with myself." She nodded and asked him how old he was. "Thousands of years old. And thousands more. I'm not as old as my father, of course, nor by older brothers, but I'm too old to remember what year it was."

And now, desperate for her brother to be safe—from what, she had no idea—she had called out to Sean and asked him for a favor. Within seconds he was with her and her dad, and she explained to him what was going on. When he left her again, to go and find her brother, she felt relief for the first time in hours.

When her phone beeped that she had a message, she looked at the text and started to cry. He was safe, and he was all right. She couldn't even speak, and handed the phone to her dad. Her friend and vampire had saved the day. Now she had to get to him and figure out what was going on. The next time her phone beeped it was from Sean.

I'm having someone look into what happened for you. She's the best there is in doing research. She told her dad and he asked if her name was Hannah Kline. *Yes, but it's Crosby now. Married to one of my brothers.*

"Hot damn, girl." Her dad danced around the room with her. "She is the best there is, and she'll find out what is happening. See if she doesn't. We'll be all right now. I promise."

Misty wasn't so optimistic as her dad was. Not that she

thought he was wrong, but no one could be that helpful, at least as helpful as the Crosby woman might be. As she packed up her things to go to Ohio, she tried to remember the last time she'd spoken to Sean. It had been years.

After he'd saved her life, they had become good friends. She would seek him out when she was lonely, and they would talk for hours on end. Then one night, she asked him why he could be out during the day and not be hurt by it.

"I'm old, for one thing, and secondly, my family and I saved the faerie queen and some of her family one night. For her thanks, she gave us this ability. We have a bit more too, but that is the reason I can be out in the sunlight." She had nodded, not sure what to believe. Sean was a jokester. "I told you I'd never lie to you, and I won't."

"You saved my life that night by killing all those men. I was terrified, but not of you, I don't think." He smiled at her and she laughed. "You've been hiding your fangs from me, haven't you?"

"I didn't want you terrified of me. And I think, a little, you are." She looked away. "I would like to ask you for something. I'd like to have a taste of your blood. That way, if you're ever in trouble again, I can find you faster. I was only walking around that area when you were hurt that night, or I wouldn't have been there for you. I'd like to be able to be there for you whenever you need it."

So tonight, when she'd heard from Alex and he told her what was going on, she'd reached for the man who could and would kill without any problem. She was so very grateful that he'd made it to Alex in time. She didn't want to lose him any more than she would have her dad. They were all she had. All she ever wanted.

Before You Go...

HELP AN AUTHOR

write a review

THANK YOU!

Share your voice and help guide other readers to these wonderful books. Even if it's only a line or two your reviews help readers discover the author's books so they can continue creating stories that you'll love. Login to your favorite retailer and leave a review. Thank you.

Kathi Barton, winner of the Pinnacle Book Achievement award as well as a best-selling author on Amazon and All Romance books, lives in Nashport, Ohio with her husband Paul. When not creating new worlds and romance, Kathi and her husband enjoy camping and going to auctions. She can also be seen at county fairs with her husband who is an artist and potter.

Her muse, a cross between Jimmy Stewart and Hugh Jackman, brings her stories to life for her readers in a way that has them coming back time and again for more. Her favorite genre is paranormal romance with a great deal of spice. You can visit Kathi online and drop her an email if you'd like. She loves hearing from her fans. aaronskiss@gmail.com.

Follow Kathi on her blog: http://kathisbartonauthor.blogspot.com/